ALSO BY MARK ALLEN

Lucas Stone/Primal Justice Series

Fury Divine

Bad Samaritan

Killing Creed

Unchained Vengeance

Savage Saints

The Assassins Series

The Assassin's Prayer

The Assassin's Betrayal

The Assassin's Resurrection

Reaper Series

Kane: Tooth & Nail (Fear the Reaper Book 1)

Kill Count

HELL'S HARVEST

LUCAS STONE
BOOK 6

MARK ALLEN

ROUGH
EDGES
PRESS

Hell's Harvest
Paperback Edition

Rough Edges Press
An Imprint of Wolfpack Publishing
1707 E. Diana Street
Tampa, FL 33610

roughedgespress.com

Paperback ISBN 978-1-68549-755-2
eBook ISBN 978-1-68549-754-5
LCCN 2026935439

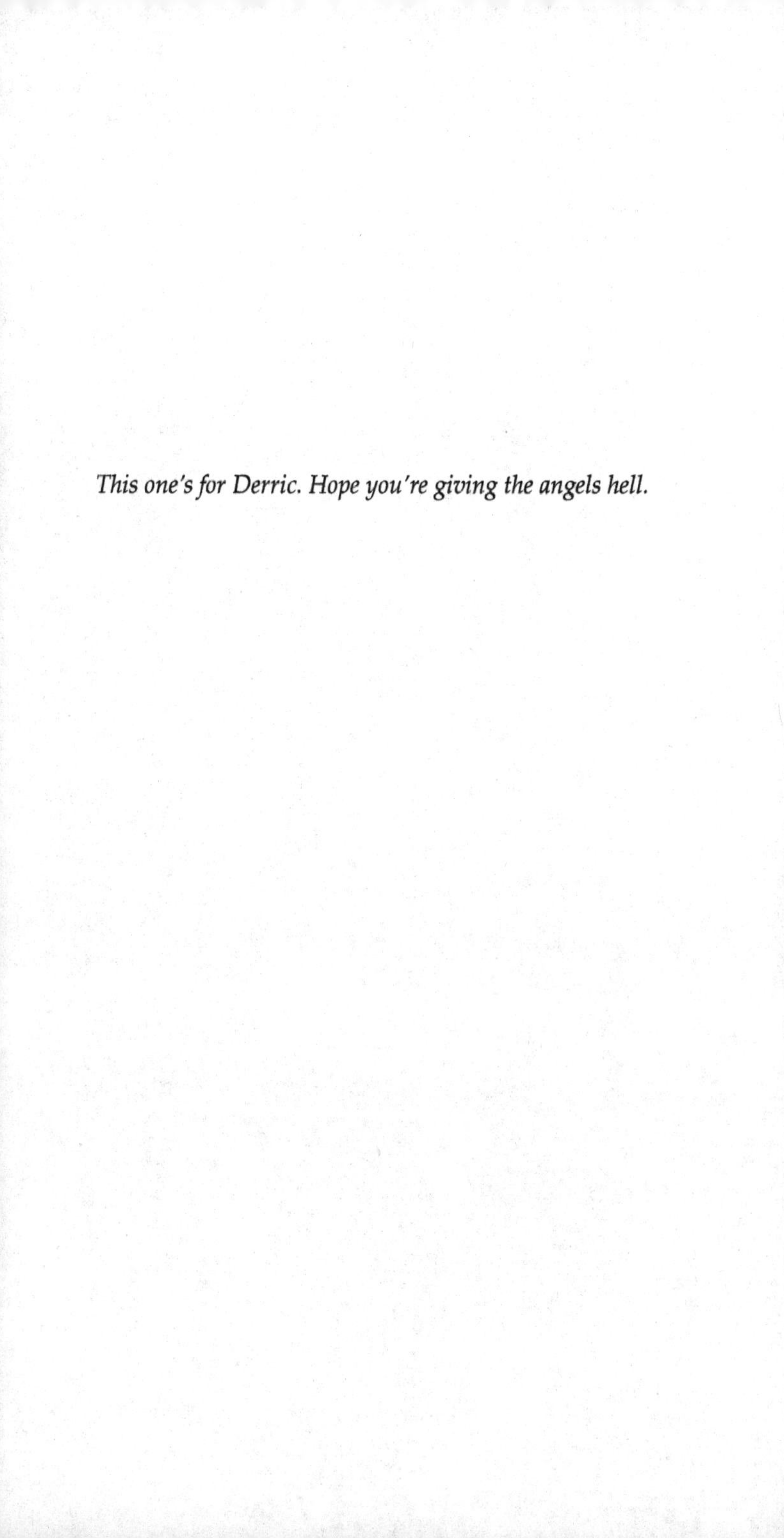

This one's for Derric. Hope you're giving the angels hell.

HELL'S HARVEST

PROLOGUE

MICHAEL DONNER, his wife Lisa, and fourteen-year-old son Carson sat at their kitchen table, together as a family, dinner spread out before them. It was their evening ritual. Maybe not quite sacred, but important enough that they tried to do it as often as possible. This being Friday night and nobody had felt like cooking, Lisa had picked up pizza and wings from the local Italian restaurant on her way home from work. Extra pepperoni on the pie, mild sauce on the chicken, with both ranch and blue cheese on the side, just the way they all liked it. There was also a two-liter of Pepsi—and a six-pack of Coors Light for Michael—to wash it all down.

Usually, they spent dinner time catching up with each other on the day's events, planning a vacation, debating politics or religion, and just generally bonding. Had anyone asked, Mike would have readily told them that they were a close-knit family and having supper together most nights was one of the reasons why, part of the glue that kept them all together.

But not tonight.

Tonight, nobody was eating.

Because instead of strengthening family bonds, they were being tortured by *actual* bonds.

Their ankles were duct-taped to the legs of their chairs, and their hands lashed together behind them with black zip ties. Mike struggled to wiggle his hands free, but their captor knew his business, and clearly, this wasn't his first rodeo. The zip ties refused to yield, digging so deep into Mike's wrists that circulation was sluggish. He could barely feel his fingers.

The pungent tang of fear-sweat permeated the room, and as Mike looked around at his family, he saw their faces filled with dread. He wondered what they saw on his face when they looked at him. If fear wasn't carved into every line of his features, it should have been—he was scared to death.

Lisa sobbed while Carson cried, but Mike tempered his fear with rage as he glared at the man who had dared to invade their home. Whisper Falls was generally one of the quieter towns in the Adirondack Mountains, but the Donners still kept their doors secured at night. But the lock on the front door had proven no match for a .45 caliber bullet. The intruder had burst in wearing a black ski mask, brandishing a 9mm automatic in one hand and a Colt .45 in the other. The handle of the Colt was made of walnut with a dragon carved into the wood, along with five notches, like an old west gunslinger marking his kills.

The two pistols were all the man needed to hold the family hostage. With guns aimed at his loved ones, Mike had done nothing as the invader bound them to the chairs, his intent still unclear. Mike just fervently prayed that whatever that intent turned out to be, murder wasn't part of the equation. Whatever else happened, no matter how horrific, Mike figured he could live with it as long as his family came out the other side still alive.

The masked man dangled the 9mm in front of Mike's face. The light from the elk antler chandelier hanging above the dining room table reflected off the stainless steel and stabbed silver flashes into Mike's eyes. The intruder waggled the pistol like a taunt as he growled, "Bet you'd like to get your grubby hands on this piece of hot lead hardware right about now, huh?"

Mike didn't reply. His look said it all.

But his look wasn't good enough for the masked man. He leaned into Mike's face until their noses were tip to tip and screamed, "Answer the question!" The man didn't articulate a threat, but he didn't need to. It was crystal clear to Mike that if he failed to answer, there would be serious consequences. He didn't even want to *think* about what those consequences might be.

"Yes," Mike whispered.

"What?" the man yelled. "Try that again, and put a little feeling behind it."

"YES!" Mike yelled back and instantly regretted it. Their captor might interpret the raised voice as defiance and shift from verbal taunts to physical punishment. *Get a hold of yourself, Mike. Don't give this maniac a reason to go kill crazy.*

"Yes…what?" the man mocked. His features were hidden under the ski mask, but Mike imagined a smirk on the prick's face.

"Yes, I'd like to have that gun right about now," Mike said, following the script. He was an actor in a dark family tragedy being directed by a madman with firepower.

The man slammed the 9mm down on the table in front of Mike so hard that several pepperonis jumped off the pizza's congealing cheese, and the salt shaker tipped over, spilling its crystalline contents.

"Well, why didn't you say so?" he asked. "It's gonna cost you, though, and the price is a real bitch."

Keeping the .45 tucked tight against Lisa's temple, the man whipped a folding knife out of his pocket. Mike experienced a marrow-freezing moment of panic as the masked man flicked open the blade, imagining the razor edge sinking into his wife's throat. But the only thing the man slashed open were the zip ties binding Mike's hands. The ease with which the plastic parted let Mike know just how sharp that knife was.

He rubbed his wrists, raw from where the straps had gouged into his flesh. The 9mm lay on the table in front of him, tantalizing, looking like lethal salvation in a polished steel package. But he knew it was an illusion. Their captor had the dragon-etched .45 pressed to his wife's head. No matter how fast Mike grabbed up the pistol, it wouldn't be fast enough to prevent the masked man from putting a bullet in Lisa's skull. So, he just left the 9mm laying there, making sure his freed hands went nowhere near it. The man seemed like he was looking for a reason to kill, and Mike didn't want to give him one.

As if to prove the point, the man suddenly ground the muzzle of the .45 into Lisa's temple and snarled, "I want to kill your wife. I want to kill her so bad that I can taste it. One little squeeze of the trigger, one little bullet tearing her pretty little head apart. God, that would feel so amazing right now."

Lisa gasped in terror. Carson began crying even harder. Mike thought his son's face looked too young to bear the horror he now faced.

"No!" Mike begged. He desperately wanted to do something, anything, to spare his family further trauma. "Please...don't."

"Well, daddy dearest, that's all up to you." The man's voice dripped with amused malice, the cat toying with the trapped mouse. "You see, I'm gonna give you a chance to save your wife."

"Anything! I'll do anything! Just please don't hurt her." Mike practically babbled his eagerness to do whatever it took, whatever the madman wanted.

"Glad to hear it," the man said. "Now, pick up the gun."

"What?"

"You heard me. I didn't stammer. Pick up the gun."

Mike glanced down at the pistol lying in front of him, then back up at the man. Back down at the gun. Back to the man.

His hesitation seemed to piss the man off. "Are you deaf?" he snarled. "You having trouble hearing the words coming out of my mouth? Let me say it slower. Pick. Up. The. Damn. Gun."

Mike's hand trembled as he obeyed the command. But once his sweaty palm gripped the cold steel, it took everything in his power not to just shoot the guy. In the movies, right about now, the hero would snap-fire a slug right between the villain's eyes, ending the terror and putting the world right once again. Cue the triumphant swell of music and roll the end credits.

But this was no movie, and he for damn sure was no hero.

"Now tuck the barrel under your chin, nice and tight," the masked man said. "Right there above that big ol' lump in your throat."

There actually *was* a lump in his throat. Mike swallowed hard and did as commanded. The metal of the gun's muzzle felt shockingly cold against his sweat-slick skin.

"Good boy," the man crooned. "Now pull the trigger."

Mike gaped at him in horror.

"NOW!" the man shouted.

Mike just sat there, frozen with fear.

"I said, now!" The man brought the .45 back—for some reason, it seemed to Mike like the dragon etched into the walnut grips was writhing like a snake—and then whipped it forward, striking Lisa across the brow. Not hard enough to knock her out, but the blow split open her skin, and blood ran down her face. She cried out in pain.

"Do it!" the man snarled. "Do it, or so help me God, I will bash your bitch's brains out all over this pizza and make the sauce extra chunky."

Mike wasn't sure when his tears had started, but he suddenly realized they were streaming down his face in a wet mockery of the blood streaking Lisa's features. *Husband and wife, 'til death do us part,* he crazily thought. *Gotta do what you gotta do.*

He slowly curled his shaking finger around the trigger and pulled it back halfway. All it would take was another three pounds of pressure to drop the firing pin on the cartridge. Another three pounds and he would feel—or, more likely, not feel—a bullet burn through his cranium. Another three pounds and he would save his wife.

But those three pounds proved impossible. His trembling finger simply refused to override his self-preservation instincts.

With the trigger locked at the halfway point, Mike let out a sigh tinged with desperation. "I can't," he said weakly. He avoided his wife's eyes, not wanting to see his shame mirrored there.

"Well, that's really bad news for the missus then," the

man said. "All right, let's keep this simple. I'm gonna rattle off a five-count. If I reach five and you haven't put a bullet through your head, I'm gonna put one through your wife's. Got it? Whether she lives or dies is entirely in your hands. Right here, right now, you are God. Life or death. The choice is all yours."

He paused to let it sink in, eyes glittering with menace behind the ski mask. Then he started the countdown. "One."

Carson struggled against his bonds as he shouted, "Dad, do something!"

Mike tried again, straining to pull the trigger. *Don't do it!* shouted the primal, reptilian side of his brain. *You have to do it!* the emotional side countered. His hand shook like a meth addict with Parkinson's. But the trigger remained static.

"Two."

Beneath the crimson streaks, Lisa's face had turned pale white. "Mike?" she whispered, voice quivering with fear.

Mike couldn't bear to look at her. He kept his eyes fixed on their tormentor. "Why are you doing this to us?" he yelled. "Why?"

The chilling answer offered no comfort. "Because it's fun. Three," he said.

"Stop! Please stop!" Mike thought he had known panic before, but it was nothing compared to the frantic horror he now felt.

"You can make me stop," the man replied. "Just pull the trigger." He paused a moment, apparently for dramatic effect, then intoned, "Four."

Mike glanced at his wife and saw a terrible serenity settle over her face, as if she had accepted her fate. Accepted the fact that her husband would not save her.

She squeezed her eyes shut and in a quiet voice murmured, "Mike, honey…"

"No no no no no no…" The single word spilled from Mike's lips again and again, his frantic mind caught in a nightmarish mental loop.

The masked man suddenly abandoned his conversational tone and switched to bellowing rage. "I'LL DO IT! I'LL PAINT THIS PLACE WITH HER BRAINS! PULL THE GODDAMNED TRIGGER! I'LL DO IT! I SWEAR TO GOD I'LL FUCKING DO IT!" His angry voice bounced off the walls and seemed to consume the room with a reverberating echo.

Carson added to the chaotic soundscape by shrieking, "Dad! Dad! Dad!"

Yet somehow, someway, in what was maybe meant to be an act of mercy from God but was anything but, Mike clearly heard Lisa's last words, *"I love you, Mike."*

He looked into her eyes and saw the forgiveness there, and his heart shattered into a thousand jagged pieces.

"Five!" his tormentor said, his tone infused with the finality of a death knell. Unlike Mike, he had no trouble pulling the trigger.

The gunshot sounded louder than the screams of ten thousand angels to Mike's stricken mind. Lisa's head snapped to the side under the hammering point-blank impact of the .45 slug. The side of her skull disintegrated and sprayed blood all over Carson's sobbing face. In a single heartbeat, with a single pull of a trigger, she was transformed from loyal wife and loving mother into a lifeless corpse.

Chuckling evilly, the masked man took the 9mm away from Mike, which was easy to do since he was just sitting there slumped in shock and horror. His mind had started shutting down, unable to process the fact that the woman he loved had just died because he had been too scared to save her. *Congratulations, Mike, you just killed your wife.*

He could take no more. His mind flicked a switch, and he slithered down the dark hole into unconsciousness.

He never saw the masked man leave or heard his final taunting words.

"Good luck getting over this one, Mikey. God hates a fucking coward."

ONE

"AND THAT," Grizzle said, "is the tragic tale of the murder of Lisa Donner."

Stone tossed back the last dregs of his drink—Jack and Coke, lots of ice, easy on the Jack—and set his empty glass down on the bar, half-melted ice cubes rattling against the sides. Like a lot of old bartenders, Grizzle was a natural storyteller, and he had spun the saga of the Donner home invasion in a way that captured Stone's attention, even though he had heard it before from other locals. He had *listened with both ears,* as his mother used to say to him in his early teen years, before she died from a brain tumor.

He had stopped by the Jack Lumber Bar & Grill at the end of a long, hot day for a post-shift drink. When he had taken the job of Garrison County Sheriff a couple years back, he had not expected there to be so much paperwork. More and more these days, he felt pinned behind his desk, buried in reports.

Adding to the misery was the fact that Valentine, his youngest deputy, had seemed totally off today, not his usual self. Clearly, something was bothering the man, but he had not offered it up, and Stone wasn't the kind to pry. He figured if the deputy wanted to talk about it, he would say so. Besides, he'd been too busy trying to dig out from under all the files burying his desk and grumbling about all the bureaucratic bullshit that came with the badge.

Maybe I should have just stuck to preaching like I originally planned, he thought, then reminded himself that it was a little late for that now.

On the way into the bar, he had passed Mike Donner heading out. Not stumbling or anything, but definitely reeking of alcohol. From Stone's understanding, that was nothing new, and not all that surprising either, given what the guy had been through. Stone had done his fair share of crawling into a bottle when his daughter died, and his marriage failed, so he could hardly blame Donner for doing the same after losing his wife in such a terrible manner. He and Mike had exchanged nothing more than polite nods, but the encounter had prompted Grizzle to launch into the whole tawdry tale while Stone drank his *Preacher*, the nickname the old black bartender had given Stone's weak, watered-down drink of choice.

"They never solved the murder, either," Grizzle said, scooping up Stone's empty glass and dumping the ice cubes in the sink. "To this day, nobody knows who that masked man was. Think if they ever found out, this town might go for an old-fashioned lynching."

A regular lawman might have said something like, "Not on my watch." But Stone was hardly a regular lawman, so he didn't bother protesting the mention of street justice.

Instead, he said, "Not sure how much effort was actually put into solving the killing. Sheriff Camden had a box full of cold case files, including the Donner murder. I skimmed all the reports when I took the job, and let's just say that my predecessor didn't appear to be pulling out all the stops to get to the bottom of the case."

Grizzle snorted. "That's 'cause Grant Camden, may he rot in hell, was a worthless, lazy jackass. I never much liked the lousy idiot even before we found out he was a raping, murdering pedophile." He gave Stone a look. "Don't let it go to your cowboy-hatted head, but you're a considerable improvement."

"You sure about that?" Stone asked. "There are some folks in town who think things got a lot more violent when I showed up." He shrugged. "I'm not even sure they're wrong."

Grizzle waved dismissively. "There's always been no shortage of violence in Garrison County. At least you handle it instead of turning a blind eye like Camden did for all those years. The fact that you deal with violence by using violence yourself, might put some people off, but I ain't one of 'em, and as you know, I hear everything at this little bar, and what I'm hearing is that the vast majority are just fine and dandy with your cowboy approach to law enforcement."

"It's the hat." Stone reached up and tapped the brim of his brown leather Stetson with the rattlesnake band, donated by the rattler responsible for his daughter's death. "Wins 'em over every time."

"A bona fide Texas yee-haw boy badging it up in northern New York." Grizzle shook his gray-haired head and smiled. "Lord knows I never thought I'd see the day."

"Yeah, well, maybe this Texas boy should take a look at the Donner case, give it a proper workup, see if I can figure things out. Might bring Mike some sort of peace, if he knew who killed his wife."

"Doubt it," Grizzle replied. "Far as Mike Donner is

concerned, *he* killed his wife when he couldn't pull the trigger. Right or wrong, he blames himself more than he blames the piece of shit that put him in that position."

"Given the circumstances, it might take a miracle to change that."

"Well, aren't you a preacher?"

"Yeah, I'm a preacher, not God."

"Guess you could at least pray for a miracle, see if God's in a giving mood," Grizzle said. "Though I doubt that'd do much to satisfy Mason Xavier."

Xavier was the richest man in the region, and it was rumored that a sizable portion of his wealth came from less than savory means. Stone had run up against him on a couple of occasions but thus far had not been able to prove anything. While he might be quick to drop the hammer on those who deserved it, Stone required evidence before putting someone in the crosshairs. So, Xavier remained free and breathing.

For now.

"What does Xavier have to do with the Donner story?" Stone asked.

"Sometimes I forget you haven't been around these parts very long," Grizzle said. "Lisa Donner was Mason's sister. Mason still carries a grudge against Mike, blames him for Lisa's death, since he didn't pull the trigger. I might not like Mason all that much, but you can hardly blame him. Not sure I'd be in a hurry to forgive the man who froze up and got my sister killed. Mason even hired a private investigator to look into the case awhile back, but no luck."

"I'll see what I can do. If I can figure out who killed Lisa Donner, maybe I can give her family some justice."

Grizzle arched an eyebrow. "Your brand of justice usually comes with a bullet attached to it."

"Some people deserve dying. Says so right in the Bible."

"Pretty sure it also says to obey the law, you cherry picker."

"You got objections to how I get things done?"

Grizzle shook his head and grinned, teeth flashing white. "No, sir, not at all. Just playing devil's advocate and screwing with you."

"I don't need you for that," Stone said. "That's what my conscience is for, and God knows it gives me enough hell."

"Then by all means, allow me to change the subject." Grizzle leaned forward, elbows on the bar, and batted his eyelashes in an exaggerated fashion. "So, how's Holly?"

"She's good," Stone said cautiously, feeling like he was being set up.

"Oh, I'll just bet she is. I'll bet she's *real* good."

"What are you implying, Griz?"

"Who, me? I'm not implying anything. Just saying that I've never seen that little lady so happy. You finally dropping the L-word on her sure did wonders for her. Makes me wonder just *how happy* you're making her." Grizzle winked and chuckled.

"Why, you looking for a little vicarious excitement?"

"Careful with the details, cowboy. My old ticker might not be able to take it."

"Maybe there aren't any details."

"Oh, there are most certainly details. No woman walks around with that kind of smile unless there are details."

"You're a dirty old man, Griz."

"Says the guy putting that smile on Holly's face."

Stone shook his head with a rueful grin and slid off the barstool.

"What, you're leaving?" Grizzle asked. "Was it something I said?"

"Things to do."

"Oh, I'll bet," Grizzle smirked. "Say hi to Holly for me."

TWO

STONE FELT the blood burning hot through his body as he and Holly kissed passionately on his couch. His Stetson sat forgotten on the coffee table next to his phone, and Holly ran her fingers through his thick, collar-length hair as she pulled him close, her velvet-soft lips crushed against his.

Max, his loyal Shepherd-Rottweiler—*Shottie*—mutt had fled from the room as soon as the make-out session began, giving them both an annoyed side-eye glare that seemed to say, *Good Lord, you two, not this crap again. I'm outta here.*

The air conditioner in the window hummed loudly to combat the August heat, but it didn't do much to cool the heat of attraction between the couple on the couch. Not even a bucket full of ice water could have done that.

Stone felt her hands slide down his neck, down his torso, under his t-shirt, and then glide back up over his muscular chest. Her fingers gently touched the scars that patchworked his skin, testament to a life lived on the killing fields. Her touch inflamed his desire, hunger surging through every nerve and synapse. He might be a preacher, but he was not the kind of preacher who believed that all physical attraction was automatically lust and therefore sinful. God created humans with urges, needs, attraction.

That being said, they weren't mindless animals either, unable to control themselves. Stone had little use for modern-day hookup culture, with sex diminished to nothing more than a few, fleeting moments of idle pleasure that meant nothing—a casual, disposable commodity briefly enjoyed, consumed, and then discarded. Stone had no use for sex without love.

And God knew he loved this woman.

Holly fell back on the couch, drawing him down with her, their lips still fused together. The short denim skirt she was wearing rode up high on her hips, and almost without thinking, Stone found his fingers opening the buttons of her blouse. The tantalizing glimpse of lace on sweat-slick skin nearly drove him crazy. She tugged off his t-shirt and dropped it on the floor.

They stayed like that for a long time, kissing and touching, half-dressed, bodies pressed together, but going no further. He managed to tear his mouth away from hers long enough to whisper, "I love you, Holly."

She smiled, and her body arched with need beneath him. She reached up, held his face gently in her hands, and gazed deep into his honey-colored eyes. "I want you, Luke. *All* of you. Right here, right now. I want to be yours." She put her lips next to his ear and whispered, "Make love to me, Luke."

Stone stared down at her, caught off guard. They'd had some pretty heavy make-out sessions over the past couple of months, but with unspoken limits. Never once had either of them suggested taking things all the way. "You sure that's what you want?" he asked.

"More than you know. It's time, Luke. I'm ready for the next step."

He didn't reply, staying silent as all sorts of emotions swirled through him.

Holly frowned at his hesitation, her brow furrowing. "What's wrong? Don't you want this?" She paused, then added, "Don't you *want me*?"

"Like you said, more than you know. I'm just..." His voice trailed off, husky with want, but laced with something else as well.

"Just...what?"

"I'm just not sure that I can."

Holly smiled up at him. "Oh, trust me, cowboy, based on what I've been feeling the last fifteen minutes, you most definitely can."

"Maybe a better way to say it is that I'm not sure I *should*."

She pushed him off and sat up, straightening her clothes, then gave him a puzzled look. Stone was grateful that she didn't look hurt or pissed or offended. She just seemed to really want to understand where he was coming from. "Mind telling me why not?" she asked. "We've officially been a couple for over a month now, not to mention the *maybe friends, maybe more* dance we did the last two years. It's not like we hopped into bed together on the first date."

Stone grinned. "Admit it, you wanted to ride me like a bronco the first time I walked into that diner and you laid eyes on me."

"Yeah, but I hid it really well."

Stone winked. "Not as well as you think."

"Seriously, Luke, tell me what's wrong."

"It's my congregation."

Holly smirked. "I was lying there with my shirt wide open and my skirt around my waist, and you were thinking about your *congregation*?" She shook her head in mock sadness. "Guess I need to work on my game some more."

Stone leaned back against the sofa cushions and sighed. "I'm a preacher, Holly. That complicates things."

"You might be a preacher, but you swear, drink, and shoot people in the face when you think they've got it coming. But sex, that's off limits? Some kind of heavenly deal breaker?"

"Well, when you put it that way, it sounds kind of stupid."

"Yeah, because it is."

On the coffee table, Stone's phone vibrated, alerting him to an incoming call. He ignored it. Whoever was calling could wait. Holly deserved his full attention.

"Listen," he said. "I'm not an orthodox preacher, that much is pretty clear by now. I don't think like a normal preacher, I don't act like a normal preacher, and for the most part, my congregation puts up with it. Most of them seem to like the fact that I'm down to earth, willing to throw out a cuss word or two, okay bellying up to the bar for a beer. The killing, well, they just seem to accept that as part of my duties as sheriff. But church people get touchy about sex—no pun intended—and most of them still believe that sex outside of marriage is a sin."

"Is that how you feel?"

"Not necessarily, but I do think it should be reserved for a loving, committed relationship."

"Isn't that what we have?"

"I think so."

"Then what's the problem?"

"The problem is that while I may be liberal with my approach on the subject, the church as a whole is not. They find out we're sleeping together, they'll most likely fire me, and I don't want to lose my church. After all the shit I did back in my past, I promised God I would become a preacher, and I came here to keep that vow."

She smirked again. "So, I'm being cockblocked by God?"

"You're such a heathen."

She ruffled her hair and sighed. "Does this mean we're never going to sleep together?"

Stone smiled. "Never say never."

His phone vibrated again, this time alerting him that the caller had left a voicemail.

"You might as well get that," Holly said. "Could be important, and it's not like we're doing anything else."

"Oh, there's plenty else we can be doing," Stone said with a wink.

"Oh, really?" Holly winked back. "Check your message and then show me what you got, cowboy."

Stone picked up his phone, swiped to his voicemail, and frowned.

Holly asked, "What's wrong?"

"The message. It's from Theresa."

"Your ex-wife?"

"Yeah."

"I thought you guys weren't in touch?"

"We're not."

"I can go to another room if you want to listen to it in private."

"I've got nothing to hide." Stone tapped the phone's touchscreen to play the voicemail. Theresa's Texas-twanged voice came from the speaker, and it was immediately obvious she was drunk.

"Luke, it's…it's Theresa. You know, your ex-wife? Ha! Of course, you know. Not like you would ever forget my voice, right? Luke, Luke, Luke, what have we done with our lives? Messed shit up, that's what we did. We had a little girl, Luke. Dear, sweet Jasmine. Gosh, she was a precious little thing,

wasn't she? Our little angel. And then she went and became a real angel and God, I couldn't forgive you for putting her on that horse even though I know it wasn't your fault."

Stone clenched his jaw so hard that he thought he might crack a molar, but he couldn't stop a tear from trickling down his cheek. All these years later, and it still hurt so damn much. He leaned forward and buried his face in his hands. Holly rested her hand on his back, warm and comforting, as Theresa continued her drunken speech.

"No, it wasn't your fault, Luke. I know that now. Truth is, I knew it way back then, back when we buried our baby girl. But I needed somewhere to put the pain, put the blame, and God help me, I put it all on you."

Stone choked back a sob as he felt old wounds tearing open, his ex-wife's words a sharp scalpel slashing at the ragged stitches of his scarred, broken heart. Dark memories surged forth like blood bubbling from a deep cut.

"It wasn't fair, Luke. What I did to you, it wasn't fair. Not even a little. Forgive me, please. Please, please, please, forgive me. Luke, I…I…well, I never should have left you. You were the one for me, the only man I ever truly loved. Jasmine's death caused more pain than I knew what to do with, but I shouldn't have pushed you away. I took our love and tossed it in the garbage like it meant nothing. But you know what, Luke? It did mean something. It meant the world, and I'd give the world right now to have it back. To have YOU back. You ever think about me? You ever have any regrets about the way things ended? Maybe, I dunno, you should have fought harder. Fought harder to keep our marriage from dying like our little girl. Fought harder not to let me push you away. How about it, Luke? Got any regrets, or is it all just me? Gosh, Theresa, what are you doing? Hang up the phone before you make a fool of yourself. Shit. Probably too late for that. Uh, sorry, Luke. I shouldn't have called. I just…I miss you sometimes. I miss US.

Letting you go was a mistake. Maybe we should fix it and give it another try. I dunno...maybe call me sometime, and we can talk about what we used to have. Who knows? God willing, maybe we can have it again."

The phone went silent, the message over.

Stone lifted his face out of his hands and looked at Holly, who was no longer rubbing his back, but sitting with arms crossed, eyes narrowed, staring at him.

"What was *that* all about?" she asked.

"Believe me, I'm as surprised as you."

"Are you?"

"I swear, the only time I hear anything from Theresa is the occasional text on the anniversary of Jasmine's death. She hasn't called me a single time since the divorce was finalized. We signed the papers and went our separate ways with barely a goodbye."

Holly started buttoning up her blouse. "Yeah, well, she clearly still carries a torch for you."

"She's just drunk, not thinking clearly."

Whether on purpose or subconsciously, while she buttoned her shirt, Holly had moved several inches away from him, ensuring there was a physical gap between them to match the emotional one that was now evolving. "How do you feel about what she said?" she asked.

"Drunken bullshit, nothing more. She'll sober up by tomorrow morning and feel like an idiot."

"Any truth to what she said?"

"Which part?"

"The part where she says she wishes your marriage had never ended, that you two had never broke up."

Stone shrugged. "I have no way of knowing how she feels."

"What about *you*?"

"What about me?"

"Do you ever think about her?"

"She's a part of my past," Stone replied. "I don't give her much thought—we split up a long time ago—but I don't want to lie to you and say she never crosses my mind."

"Do you miss her?"

"I barely think about her."

"You didn't answer the question."

Stone shook his head. "You're trying to pick a fight. I'm not playing that game."

"You have to look at it from my point of view, Luke. Five minutes ago, you refused to sleep with me even though I was throwing myself at you, and now your ex-wife calls begging for you guys to get back together."

"One thing's got nothing to do with the other."

"I'd really like to believe that."

"Then believe it and let's move past this."

"Not sure I can."

Stone stared at her. "Are you serious?"

Her arms remained folded across her chest. She looked hurt and unsure and angry, and Stone desperately wished he could make all those emotions go away. *Damn you, Theresa.*

"You'd never lie to me, right, Luke?" Holly asked.

"Of course not."

"So, tell me the truth: did you want your marriage to end?"

"It wasn't my idea, no."

"So, your wife stopped loving you. You didn't stop loving your wife."

"We both drifted away from each other after Jasmine died," Stone said. "She just happened to be the one who called it quits first."

Holly stared at him, suspicious eyes roving his face, searching for the truth. He met her gaze levelly, knowing full well he had nothing to hide. "Tell me something," she finally said. "If we weren't together right now and you got that message, what would you do?"

"I don't know," he said, keeping it honest. "But what-ifs don't help anything. Theresa is my past, and there's nothing I can do about that. We all have pasts, and they're not always pretty. But *you* are my present. I love *you*, Holly, not Theresa."

"I want to believe that," she said. "I really do. But the fact that you're not sure you wouldn't call her back if I wasn't in the picture tells me a lot, and it should tell you something too." She stood up, smoothed her skirt, and headed for the door. "I think you need to make sure your past is really behind you before we can have a relationship."

Stone was stunned. "Are you breaking up with me?"

"I don't know what you want to call it, but we're taking some time off. Looks like we both have a lot of thinking to do, a lot of shit to figure out."

"Holly..."

But she was gone, the door slamming shut behind her.

THREE

THAT EVENING, as the sun began to sink in the sky and impale itself on the pointed peaks of the Adirondack Mountains, deep in the darkest, most remote corner of the Scar Lake region, a young woman sat cross-legged, hands cupped in front of her, holding a black and yellow Joro spider. She had been pretty once, and maybe still was—she hadn't seen a mirror in a very long time. But even without a mirror, she knew that any prettiness that might remain was buried beneath the dirt and filth and abuse, like a sapphire covered in dung.

Her home—well, prison, actually—was a ramshackle cabin that was little more than a large, dilapidated shed. She was taken outside once every two weeks to bathe in the icy stream nearby, so she knew that the cabin squatted in a small hollow, ringed by massive boulders. She also knew there were a lot of bodies and bones buried in the ground around the place, and sometimes they made their way to the surface. Last week, during her bimonthly trip to the cold creek, she had glimpsed a half-rotted skull grinning out from the dirt, black sockets brimming with worms and secrets.

On the south side of the cabin, her captors had erected a makeshift lean-to, which looked like it would collapse under the weight of the snow in the winter, but for some reason never did. A pair of large coolers perched there, powered by a generator that ran constantly since no electrical lines ran this far back in the wilderness. Heavy logging chains, thick with rust, draped the coolers like old, fallen cobwebs. Portable propane tanks clustered together in the corner. Crows often perched on the edge of the lean-to, waiting to scavenge morsels of meat from the garbage. The black carrion-eaters seemed to think of the place as their personal feeding ground and skulked around like dark-winged shadows.

Inside the cabin, as the setting sun burnished the sky with a coppery tint, the woman stared at the walls around her. They had been her only view for so long, she knew every inch of them like the back of her hand. They were fashioned from rough-hewn timber and looked like they might have been painted white once, but now they were mostly just bare. Same with the floor, which consisted of wooden boards with some threadbare throw rugs scattered around.

The kitchen area featured a small gas stove and refrigerator. There was a wood stove in the corner as well, with a kettle on top that was so large, it looked like it should be surrounded by a coven of cackling witches brewing and bubbling some kind of cursed concoction. But in actuality, it was just used to heat water. The woman actually would have preferred evil witches to the savage men who kept her captive here.

One large, stainless-steel table with rough-chopped logs for legs dominated the center of the room. Dark stains turned the floor beneath a deep, rust-brown color.

The table was where the horror happened. The blood, the screams, the butchery.

The woman lived in a padlocked dog kennel, eight feet long, five feet wide, six feet tall, with nothing but a dirty mattress and an equally dirty blanket. She ate here, slept here, suffered abuse here...though sometimes they took her out of the cage to torment her. Never sexually—their abuse was always about the infliction of pain. Three of the four men were cutters, taking sadistic pleasure in slicing open her flesh and watching her bleed. The fourth, the biggest, preferred to use his fists, getting his rocks off through black-and-blue beatings. Her slim body bore a patchwork of scars, a cruel testimony to the hell she had endured since being brought here.

This was her life now—imprisoned, caged, trapped in an endless cycle of hurt and torment, with no hope of escape. She looked down into her cupped hands at the large but harmless Joro spider sitting calmly in her palm. When you're living in a nightmare, sometimes your friends come in strange forms. At least she was only talking to bugs, not eating them. "Forever, Mr. Joe," she whispered to her eight-legged companion. "That's how long they've kept me in this cage. I don't know how much more I can take..."

Her voice trailed off as she looked down at her body, which bore more signs of suffering than she could even count. Dressed in tattered clothes that were little more than rags, the scars were starkly visible and easy to see, a map of misery carved into her flesh.

She leaned over and raised the spider up to her face. "I know I couldn't have made it this far without you," she said. "You're my eight-legged angel." She almost kissed the spider, but thought better of it. When your makeshift best friend is a large arachnid, some boundaries are best left uncrossed.

A stick snapped outside. The woman shivered. They were back. Her precious moments of peace were over.

"Hurry, Mr. Joe, they're coming! Go! Go! Go!" The spider responded to her urgent voice and darted out of the cage, scuttling across the floor to run up to the wall to the darkest corner of the cabin, where it settled in the center of its web.

The cabin door banged open, and the woman immediately began to tremble. She lived in hell, and now the devils had come home.

She had given them all nicknames. The leader of the group—she called him Honcho—stomped in first. He stood at least six-foot-two, maybe taller, his face heavily pocked with acne damage that gave him a menacing look. He glanced at her dispassionately, and she glimpsed the predatory intelligence glittering in his gaze. He was the *head honcho*—hence the nickname—of the killer pack, the one who called the shots on a day-to-day basis. The actual mastermind behind this brutal operation rarely bothered to make an appearance, apparently content to let Honcho call the shots during his prolonged absences. Honcho carried a sawed-off shotgun over his shoulder, dangling from a leather sling.

Behind him loomed the man she called Goliath, a muscle-bound brute who looked like a massive NFL linebacker jacked up on steroids. Easily six-foot-six with a pumpkin-sized head and beady, soulless eyes set in a heavily bearded face. His prominent jaw thrust forward, giving him a serious underbite that had probably earned him a fair share of bullying in school. No gun, but he carried a hatchet in a leather sheath on his belt. She had witnessed him using it to split wood, flesh, and bone, and knew he kept the edge well-honed.

Patch and Doc were the last to enter the cabin. Patch was bald, his head dappled with sweat from the summer heat, and wore a black patch over his right eye. The woman had only seen him without it once, just a fleeting glimpse that revealed nothing remained behind the path but a stitched-up socket. His left eye was a brilliant blue, like crystal ice, and just as cold. He wore a short-barreled, stainless-steel revolver on his left hip, and while the woman didn't know much about guns, she had heard it referred to as a .357 Magnum. She had watched Patch shoot someone point-blank in the head with it once, and the bullet blew out the whole side of the victim's skull, so she knew it was a powerful weapon, at least at close range. Maybe she would get lucky and somehow manage to get her hands on it one day. It would be a whole lot better to hold a gun than a spider. But she had long ago given up hoping for miracles.

Doc was the most normal-looking of the bunch, smaller than the others, with the long, thin, steady fingers of a pianist or surgeon. She had lost track of how many times she had watched those fingers wield a scalpel, carving the organs out of countless victims so they could be sold on the black market. Or, worse, filleting strips of human meat to sell to the eccentric billionaire up in Canada who apparently had a cannibalism fetish. *"Sick freak claims it tastes like pork,"* she'd once overheard Honcho tell the others. *"Guess they even call it long pig."*

Doc glanced her way as he entered the cabin, his eyes raking over her body. He gave her a little grin, and she shuddered, fear pulsing through her. Many of her scars had come from Doc's scalpel during *playtime*. She looked away, desperately hoping that they didn't haul her out of the cage tonight for their twisted idea of fun.

I should just kill myself, she thought for the thousandth—maybe millionth—time since her abduction. *Find a way to cut my wrists, or bite off my own tongue and bleed to death.*

But she never did. Never even tried. Not just because she believed suicide was a sin—though that definitely played a part—but because she possessed a deep-rooted will to survive. Yes, killing herself would rob these pricks of the thrill of torturing her, but it would also mean they had broken her. She refused to give them that satisfaction. Hell, no. Was she desperate? Sure. But not desperate enough to die.

Not yet, anyway.

It was amazing how long you could live in terror. How long you could just keep on going, keep on surviving, even after you felt God had abandoned you.

Patch grabbed a hard-boiled egg from the refrigerator. He tossed it back and forth in his hands for a moment like a baseball, then dragged a chair over to the table, sat down, and started peeling the shell. He glanced over at the cage as he worked and called out, "Hey, we got time to play with the little lady? She's looking like she needs some of my special attention."

The woman cowered in fear. *No, no, no, no…*

"Don't you ever get tired of messing with her?" Honcho asked, rolling his eyes. He was sitting in a chair in the corner, reading an old horror paperback.

"What else is there to do, for god's sake? We're back here in the middle of bumfuck nowhere."

"You're getting paid, aren't you?"

"Doesn't mean I can't have some fun during the downtime."

Honcho shrugged and went back to his book. "Whatever floats your boat, man. Just remember the rules: you can't screw her, you can't kill her, and no permanent injuries."

"Can't believe we obey that don't-fuck-her rule," Patch grumbled. "Like, how would the big boss even know? He barely comes around."

"When he does show up, she'd tell him," Honcho said, over the top of his paperback.

Patch snorted. "You never heard of lying? Who's the boss man gonna believe, us or her?"

"He's got a knack for sniffing out the truth and zero tolerance for rule breakers," Honcho replied. "We've got a good thing going here, and I'm not screwing it up because you want to get your rocks off."

"No worries." Patch popped the peeled egg in his mouth whole, chewed, and swallowed. "I'll just make the bitch bleed a little." He brushed the cracked shell into his hand, went to the trash to throw it away, and then approached the cage.

The woman knew screaming wouldn't help anything, but she couldn't stop herself. Her cries reverberated off the walls, bouncing back in the form of futile echoes. "No, please! Don't! Please!"

Patch ignored her pleas and then reached into the cage, grabbed a fistful of hair, and dragged her out. She struggled as he wrenched her across the floor, arms flailing, legs kicking, but she was no match for his strength. He picked her up and slammed her down on the table. Her spine jarred from the violent impact, and pain radiated through her body like fingers of fire.

But she knew it was nothing compared to the pain about to come.

She didn't bother begging for mercy as Patch went to work on her. She just suffered and bled and wondered why God had allowed her to fall into the clutches of these monsters. She felt the pain but tried to distance herself from it, and tried to force herself into a state of shock. She begged her consciousness to contract, for blackness to take her vision, but it didn't happen. She felt every slice of the blade, the liquid heat of her blood spilling, the vile laughter of the man cutting her for no other reason than his own sadistic amusement.

She began to pray, out loud, the same words over and over. Not because she believed it would help, but because there was nothing else she could do. "The Lord is my shepherd, I shall not want...the Lord is my shepherd, I shall not want...the Lord is my shepherd..." She squeezed her eyes shut for a moment, as if that would help her desperate supplications reach beyond the ceiling rafters.

When she opened them, Patch was leaning over her.

"Save your prayers and shut your mouth," he growled. "Or I'll fetch the chainsaw and blowtorch and show you a real good time." He spat in her face. "Ain't no God here, bitch."

Maybe not, she thought. *But the devil sure is.*

And then the world dissolved into darkness and pain.

FOUR

STONE SLEPT like shit and seriously contemplated becoming a monk. That seemed pretty appealing right about now. Check himself into a monastery, take a vow of chastity, and be done with the complications of emotions and desires and relationships. Just him and God.

Then again, he thought, *when you get right down to it, it's always just you and God.*

He had resisted the nearly overwhelming temptation to call Holly—she said she wanted some space, so he would respect that, even if he didn't like it one damn bit—and instead had gone to bed early. Which had turned out to be a colossal waste of time, since all he did was toss and turn and think about Holly. And if he was being truthful, about Theresa. God knew there was a whole lot of history there. But that's all it was—history. He just needed to convince Holly of that.

Easier said than done.

He had given up on sleep and crawled out of bed before dawn had even cracked a splinter of light across the sky. A quick shower rinsed off the night-sweat and then he drove down to Faith Bible Church to work on his sermon for tomorrow morning's worship service. More and more these days, he found himself waiting until the last minute to hammer out a message for the congregation. While he hated to admit it, he knew deep down that his duties as sheriff were taking a toll on his duties as a preacher. He was guilty of prioritizing the former at the expense of the latter. The scripture verse that talked about how no man can serve two masters came to mind.

Yeah, that's me these days. The Bible taking a backseat to the badge.

Confession might be good for the soul, but this one, even though it was silent, troubled him. He needed to do better because God deserved better. Looked like his relationship with Holly wasn't the only thing in his life that was out of alignment.

He'd been scribbling on a notepad, making sermon notes for several hours when he heard someone call out from the main sanctuary. "Hello? Pastor Stone? Saw your truck out front and thought you might be here."

Stone didn't recognize the voice. No surprise whoever it was thought he was here, though—his truck was a '78 Chevy Blazer with the sheriff's department logo painted on the door and a red-and-blue LED light bar on the roof, so not exactly low profile. "Back here in my office," he said loudly. While he doubted any of his enemies would announce their presence, his hand still slid open a desk drawer and rested next to the Colt Cobra .38 snub-nosed revolver hidden there, nestled next to the leatherbound Bible his father had given him. Better safe than sorry. The fact that he was a preacher who needed to keep a gun within arm's reach said a lot about him, he thought.

A moment later, a man appeared in the office doorway, and Stone recognized Perry Burke, the minister over at Good Shepherd Nazarene Church in Bloomingdale. Stone immediately relaxed and closed the desk drawer.

Burke posed no threat. With his thinning hair, middle-aged paunch, and tweed sport coat, Burke looked more like a professor than a preacher. Someone who should be pontificating on the phallic symbolism of Moby Dick to a college literature class rather than pounding a pulpit.

"Morning, Perry," Stone greeted. "Come on in, have a seat."

Burke walked over and sat down in one of the chairs arranged in front of the desk. He rested his hands on his knees as he spoke. "Sorry to bother you so early. Like I said, I was driving by and saw the truck, so thought it might be a good time to swing in."

"No bother at all," Stone said, leaning back in his chair. "What brings you my way?"

Burke didn't look nervous, but something heavy lurked behind his eyes, something that had not been there the last time Stone saw him, which had been at an ecumenical prayer breakfast at the Adirondack Community Church over in Lake Placid a couple of months ago. Then again, the man had every right to look burdened and sorrowful. His seventeen-year-old daughter, Jenny, had been mauled to death by a bear a little over a year ago while hiking in the Scar Lake region, a remote, rugged wilderness area northwest of Garrison County, not much more than a stone's throw from the Canadian border. Having a soft spot for fathers who had lost their daughters in tragic accidents, Stone had attended her funeral, which had, by necessity, been a closed-casket service.

"I've been dropping by all the churches in the area," Burke said. "Letting the pastors know about something I feel God has led me to do."

"I'm listening."

Burke rubbed his palms on his pants, as if his hands were sweaty. "As you know, my daughter, Jenny, died last year." He tilted his head, a sympathetic look on his face. "If I recall correctly, we have that particular pain in common."

Stone nodded. Between Theresa's drunken message last night and now Burke's visit, he was remembering Jasmine's death more than usual. It still hurt like hell. Time heals all wounds was a bullshit lie, and Stone knew that all too well. Time didn't heal anything, it just made the pain a little easier to live with.

"Yeah, that's a pain you never really get over," Burke said, almost as if he had read Stone's mind. "It took me quite a while to understand that it's never really going to go away." He gave Stone a small, commiserating smile. "But I suppose you know that already."

Stone nodded again. "You learn to live with it. But that doesn't mean it stops hurting."

"Well, I want something good to come from all that pain," Burke said. "The Good Lord's been nudging me to pull something holy out of the ashes, to make Jenny's death mean something, to give it a purpose and a reason."

Stone didn't say anything. He knew he was more cynical—though he preferred the term *realistic*—than most preachers and believed that sometimes death just happened, that sometimes the innocent died for no good reason at all, the consequences of living in a fallen world. *"The Lord works in mysterious ways"* was clichéd as hell, but like all cliché sayings, it was rooted in the truth, because it was an absolute mystery to Stone why his daughter, or Burke's daughter, had needed to die.

But if Burke found some comfort in fashioning meaning out of Jenny's death, far be it from Stone to stop him. Sure, he could be cold and factual at times, but he tried not to be cruel, especially to those in grief.

"I own a small cabin up in Scar Lake, really more of a

hunting camp," Burke said. "It's a quiet place, very simple, about a mile back in the woods, give or take. After Jenny's death, I started using it as something of a mission outreach for people in my church, a secluded place for people who needed to get away from it all, to be alone with God, to heal."

"Sounds like a great idea," Stone said.

"So, what I'm doing is going around and offering it to all the other pastors in the area. If you have any church members who you think would benefit from using the cabin, they're more than welcome. First come, first served, of course." Burke smiled. "It's meant to be an impromptu spiritual retreat for when the need arises, not a formal Airbnb setup."

"Sounds like you're taking your sorrow and turning it into sanctuary," Stone said. "Well done."

"Like I said, I'm just doing what the Lord told me to do."

"Can't ever go wrong doing that." Stone leaned forward and clasped Burke's hand firmly. "Thanks for this, Perry. If I come across someone I think would benefit from your offer, I'll definitely give you a call."

Burke's grip was steady. "Thanks for your time, Luke." He stood up, gave Stone a farewell nod, and left the office. Stone thought there was something resolute about the man, a strength not immediately obvious from his professor-like demeanor.

Burke had suffered hell but had emerged from the flames with grace and compassion and an interest in building something from the ashes. He had taken his pain and turned it into purpose. Stone respected that.

Some people just say they're following God, but Burke actually lives it. Talk about faith in action.

Stone tore up his sermon notes and started over.

FIVE

THE NEXT MORNING, Stone was back in his church office a full hour before the Sunday worship service started. The sermon, inspired by his conversation with Perry Burke, was good and ready to go, but Stone himself looked like dog crap left on the side of the road in the hot sun and then run over by a steamroller. Another night of no sleep had left his eyes so burning that not even liberal doses of Visine were getting the red out. He wondered if he could get away with preaching the sermon with his sunglasses on.

Holly still wasn't returning his calls and was ignoring his text messages. He could see that she was reading them, but no response. Part of him felt like she was over-reacting, but the other part couldn't really blame her. She'd had a rough go with romance in the past, and that had put her heart on guard for a whole lot of years. And now, just when she finally lowered her defenses and dared to love again, a blindside shot from his ex-wife came out of nowhere and struck a blow. Stone didn't have to like it, but he couldn't deny that Holly had a right to be rattled.

Just give her more time. She'll come around.

That's what Stone told himself anyway, and he hoped it was the truth. But he imagined if he had said that to Max this morning, the dog would have rolled his eyes and given him a look that said, *Yeah, you keep on believing that shit, man, and good luck to ya. Don't forget to give me a biscuit before you leave.*

Stone shook his head ruefully and went into the private bathroom to splash some cold water on his face and hope to God it helped. He needed to pull himself together before he preached, which was in about an hour. Showing up looking like hammered roadkill would give Deacon White one more reason to despise him. Not that Stone particularly cared all that much.

When he came out of the bathroom, Lizzy was sitting in one of the chairs in front of the desk, chewing bubblegum and giving him an appraising—and slightly disapproving—stare. She crossed her arms and without preamble, asked, "So, what did you do to my mom?"

The fact that she had managed to enter his office without detection let Stone know just how mentally distracted he was these days. He wasn't operating at peak performance levels, and if Lizzy had been an enemy, he would be dead right now. "Who says I did anything to your mom?" he asked, trying to buy some time.

"Oh, don't give me that crap." Lizzy blew a bubble and popped it. The color of the gum matched the purple streaks in her black hair, which was pulled into a ponytail. "Mom's been mega-happy ever since you came back from Mexico and professed your undying love and affection. Then she goes to your place two nights ago and comes back crying and angry and miserable." The teenager tilted her head. "So, I'd say it's pretty obvious that you did something to my mom. You gonna tell me what happened?"

Stone sat on the edge of his desk. "What'd she tell you?"

"She didn't tell me *anything*. Heck, I've barely even seen her since she came home that night. She disappeared into her room with a bottle of wine and didn't bother bringing a glass. That's why I'm asking you what's up."

"It's complicated," Stone said.

"That's such a cheap-ass answer."

"Maybe, but it's the truth."

"Yeah, well, life is complicated."

"What makes you say that?" Stone asked. "You got complications of your own?"

"Just nervous about senior year of high school, is all." She popped out of the chair, circled behind the desk, and spit her gum directly in the wastebasket.

Stone couldn't help but smile. That was Lizzy for you. All girly and feminine one moment, and rough as rocks the next. She had been through a lot of shit in her young life, so it wasn't exactly surprising that a hard edge revealed itself sometimes. "What's there to be nervous about?" he asked.

She shuffled back to the front of the desk and slumped back down in the chair. "Nothing. Never mind. Forget I said anything."

"C'mon, Liz, don't be like that."

"You'll just laugh at my teenage girl angst."

"Right. Because I always laugh when you tell me stuff."

"All right, fine, I'll give you that," she said. "You're actually a pretty good listener."

"Comes with the territory. Can't be worth much as a preacher if you can't listen to people when they have problems. So, tell me about yours."

Lizzy let out a long, heavy sigh. "It's just all the senior year shit, you know? I mean, I know I'm supposed to be excited—and I am, don't get me wrong. No more school? What's not to like, right? But there's all this pressure that comes with it. It's like, a year from now, I'm supposed to have my life all figured out. What do I want to do for a career? What about college? What's my future look like?" She shook her head. "And when all that crap goes crashing through my mind, all I can think is, what if I mess it all up?"

Stone looked at her, his gaze steady. From the very beginning, when he had caught her smoking behind a bar after a fight with her mom, their relationship had been built on trust, without unnecessary bullshit and sugar-coating. "I get it," he said. "It's a lot, and I won't pretend that it isn't. But since it's Sunday, I'm going to pretend I'm some kind of half-assed preacher—"

"Half-assed at best," she interrupted with a smile.

"—and tell you that there's a verse in the Bible that tells us not to worry about tomorrow because there's enough shit to worry about today."

"What the heck version is that?"

"I may have paraphrased." Stone grinned. "But the point still stands."

"Sounds good and all," Lizzy said. "But as you know, I'm not really much of a Bible thumper."

"So let me take another shot, this time without the preacher tactics."

"Go for it."

"Since when have you been someone who lets fear control you?" Stone asked, pointed and direct. "God knows you've been through a whole lot worse than anything senior year is gonna throw at you."

Lizzy barked out a sharp, humorless laugh. "God, ain't that the truth."

"Right," Stone said. "And you're still kicking."

"I don't know." Lizzy shrugged. "Somehow, for

some reason, this just feels, I dunno...different. Everything's changing. I mean, think about it, I might not even *be* here this time next year. High school is the end of an era. After graduation, nothing will ever be the same again. So many choices to make, choices that can define the rest of my life. What if I take the wrong road?"

Stone could hear the emotion in her voice. It was tucked away—Lizzy didn't usually wear her heart on her sleeve—but he knew her well enough that he could sense it. "We all make bad choices sometimes," he said. "No matter who you are, you'll look back at some decisions you made in life and wish you had done things differently. Regret is just part of life."

"Well, aren't you just a big ol' bundle of encouragement." She quirked up the corner of her mouth to let him know she was just teasing.

"Listen, if it'll make you feel better, after church I'll go buy you a Hallmark card and a teddy bear."

"Okay, now you're just being hurtful."

They shared a smile and then Stone said, "Listen, Lizzy, you have to remember that you're not going through this alone. You've got people in your life who love you and who will be there no matter where you go, what you do, or where you end up. If you can't have faith in anything else, have faith in that."

"That include my mom?"

"Of course it does."

"That include you?"

"Absolutely."

"That include you and my mom...*together*?"

"I hope so, but we've got some things to figure out."

"Well, then, you need to figure it out." The look she gave him was both piercing and pleading. "You're the guy who's always making things right. Well, make *this* right. Whatever happened between you and my mom, fix it."

"It's not that easy," Stone said.

"I don't care if it's easy or not," Lizzy replied. "It just needs to get fixed. Don't screw this up, Luke. I can't lose you. You're the only *dad* I've got left."

Stone swallowed the sudden lump in his throat. He had tried hard to just be Lizzy's friend and not selfishly turn her into a replacement for his dead daughter. But hearing her call him *dad* warmed a place deep inside him, way beyond the meat and marrow, that he had feared might forever remain cold and hollow. It was especially heartening since last year he had been forced to gun down her real father, a Vegas mob boss, after he escaped from prison and came looking for Holly with brutal vengeance on his mind. Lizzy had witnessed the shooting with her own eyes, and Stone had feared that, despite how evil her father was, she might never forgive him for putting a bullet in the man's head.

But she had made it clear, even before today, that she held no grudge.

She really was one hell of a kid.

Lizzy stood up, walked over, and curled her arms around him in a quick hug. "I mean it, Luke. You need to fix things with Mom."

Stone hugged her back. "I'll see what I can do."

SIX

MIKE DONNER SAT ALONE in the front pew of Faith Bible Church, staring up at the large wooden cross that adorned the wall behind the pulpit. This being a Protestant church—well, independent nondenominational if you wanted to put a name on it—rather than Catholic, the cross was just a cross, not a crucifix. There was no impaled Christ, and for that, Mike was thankful. He understood the whole *Jesus died on the cross for the sins of the world* thing, but there had been more than enough blood and violence in his life, so he was glad that he didn't have to come to church on Sunday and look at an innocent man nailed to a hunk of wood.

Not that he went to church much these days.

A purple banner stretched above the cross and greeted anyone who entered the sanctuary with *Welcome to Faith Bible Church*. It was a simple banner and a simple greeting, but this was a simple mountain town church. It had gained some notoriety over the last couple of years when Pastor Lucas Stone took over, his earthy, unorthodox approach to faith and preaching winning over a lot of folks. Not to mention his gun-blazing, one-man-army takedown of a survivalist compound that had been raping and murdering little girls. It wasn't very often you met a preacher with a kill-count.

Mike idly wondered how many of the people attending the church these days were here solely for the novelty of listening to a preacher who cussed, drank, and carried a gun and wasn't afraid to use it. Growing up here, it had always been his opinion that Whisper Falls wasn't a particularly religious town and that most of those who bothered to attend church viewed it more as a social gathering than anything related to true faith.

Not that there was anything wrong with that. In his experience, true faith usually just ended up in bitter disappointment. He hadn't seen much evidence that God came through when the chips were down.

Mike sat on the pew and listened to the congregants in the foyer as they headed home for Sunday dinners with family, voices full of hope and joy, a stark contrast to the bleak and blackened thoughts scorching his own mind. It was probably good that his neighbors couldn't see the darkness caged within him. He didn't hate them or anything like that, but he sometimes couldn't help but resent them for their normalcy.

But while he might not have hated his neighbors, there *was* someone that he had learned to hate, someone very deserving, as far as he was concerned.

Staring up at the cross, Mike whispered, "You bastard, you let me kill her."

A hand gripped his shoulder. Mike jumped up out of the pew and spun around, fists raised for combat or defense. His heart rate immediately doubled, jackhammering in his chest.

Stone held up his hands with his palms out to show

he meant no threat. "It's just me, Mike." The preacher wore jeans, boots, and a forest-green polo shirt. In keeping with his unorthodox methods, Stone rarely donned a suit to preach. He believed God cared about the heart, not the clothes.

Mike lowered his arms. "Sorry, preacher. You caught me off guard, with my head somewhere else."

"No need to apologize to me, but you may want to say sorry to God for calling Him a bastard."

"You heard that, huh?"

"I heard it. But don't worry, I'm not judging. We all have our moments where God's not our favorite person."

"Yeah, me and God aren't exactly on the best of terms these days," Mike said. "I'm kind of holding a grudge over the whole dead wife thing."

"Good thing is, God's big enough to handle our grudges. Whenever you're ready to patch things up, He'll be waiting."

Let it go, preacher. Mike felt himself getting agitated. He made a noise in his throat that was close to a growl. "It's not always that simple," he said. "God or not, sometimes life just sucks." He almost added the word *dick* but caught himself at the last second. Not that the cussing clergyman would have cared.

Stone smiled. "Life sucks... That would make a good sermon title, actually." Then he turned more serious. "Honestly, Mike, I get where you're coming from. I know a thing or two about going through rough shit."

Mike nodded. The fact that Stone had lost his daughter in Texas was no secret around Whisper Falls. He didn't talk about it much, except maybe to that Holly Bennett woman he was always hanging around with, but there was no doubt that Stone had his own tragic cross to bear. He and Mike both had graves to visit.

I wonder if he drinks away the pain every night, too.

"Difference is," Mike said, "that rattlesnake bit your daughter's horse before you had a chance to do anything about it. You didn't have the option of saving her. I can't say the same thing about Lisa."

"You were faced with an impossible choice."

"Shouldn't have been a choice at all," Mike snapped. "The only reason it was impossible is because I'm a damned coward. Emphasis on the word *damned*."

"Mike, listen—"

But Mike put up his hand to cut him off. "No offense, preacher, but I really don't want to talk about it anymore."

"Okay, what *do* you want to talk about? I assume there's a reason you're still hanging around."

"Got a problem, figured a preacher might be able to help me through it, bumped into you at the Jack Lumber the other night, and figured your church was as good as any, so I showed up today."

"Happy to help," Stone said. "Tell me about your problem."

Mike looked down at his feet, shoulders slumped. "My son Carson. He gets out of jail—well, juvenile detention—tomorrow. I have to pick him up at eleven." Just saying his son's name made Mike hurt in ways he couldn't even begin to describe. Lisa might have been the one who died that horrible night, but she wasn't the only victim. "Since he was sentenced as a minor, they could only hold him until he was eighteen, which he turned yesterday."

Stone nodded. "Makes sense. The sins of our youth shouldn't be held against us. He got any remorse for his actions?"

Mike shrugged. "Hard to say. He was pretty bitter when they put him away."

"So, what happens next?" Stone asked. "For the two of you, I mean."

"He's my son," Mike replied. "Nothing I would like more than to put this rough patch behind us. I can't bring his mother back, but maybe he and I could have some kind of a fresh start."

Stone reached over and placed an encouraging hand on Mike's shoulder. "Good to hear. Everyone deserves a second chance."

"Yeah, that's what I wanted to talk to you about. I'm kind of at a loss on how to move forward with Carson."

"When's the last time you saw him?"

Mike lowered his head again, as if the floor of the sanctuary held answers to the problems of his life, and said, "The day he went to juvie."

"They locked him up three years ago, and you never went to visit him?"

Mike looked up with a pained, cynical smile. "Oh, I went. Every Saturday morning, religiously. But he refused my visits. Every single one of them." He sighed, long and heavy. "My son hates me and that's all there is to it." Though he had faced that heartbreaking fact a long time ago, it was the first time Mike had uttered the words aloud. It felt like a confession…a confession that hurt like hell.

Stone seemed to reach some kind of decision. "I think I can help," he said. "Pastor Burke over at the Nazarene church lets people use his hunting cabin up in Scar Lake to get away and try to find some healing. Why don't you and Carson head up there for a few days, do some varmint hunting, some fishing, try to reconnect?"

Mike smiled. It felt out of place on his face. "Not a bad idea. Thanks, I appreciate it. Not sure it'll do much good, but it's worth a try."

"Don't underestimate the power of some father-son

time in the woods," Stone said. "Hell, most of the time, I feel closer to God in the woods than I do in church."

The more Mike thought about the idea, the more he liked it. Get away from civilization, spend some quality one-on-one time with Carson, and see if they could start to rebuild some kind of bond. Some roaring bonfires, some grilled food, maybe a few cold beers, and some heart-to-heart chats to start dealing with their emotional trauma. Maybe they wouldn't make it all the way back to reconciliation in just one trip, but any journey started with the first step.

"I really appreciate you setting this up for us," he said.

"When do you want to go?" Stone asked.

"The sooner the better. Like, tomorrow, if you can make it happen."

"I'll call Burke this afternoon and set it up, then drop by your place later and give you the key. Sound good?"

"Sure does." Mike stood up, and the two men shook hands. "Thanks, preacher."

"No problem. And call me Luke."

As Mike headed down the aisle toward the exit, he glanced over his shoulder at the cross he had so recently cursed. He considered offering up an apology, but then shook his head.

Nah. Not a chance.

Outside, he stood at the bottom of the church steps for a moment and enjoyed the warm summer air kissing his skin. The sun burned high and bright in a sky that was clear save for a few cotton puffs of clouds above the mountain peaks. It was the kind of day that made you want to jump on a boat and go cruising across a lake with a drink in your hand. Of course, he rarely needed much of an excuse to have a drink in his hand.

He breathed deeply, inhaling the fresh breeze and the

scent of wildflowers it carried, then moved across the parking lot at a brisk clip. Since Pastor Stone's Chevy was parked behind the church, Mike's Jeep Wrangler was the only vehicle left out front.

The Jeep was *murdered out,* meaning it was black from roof to rims. He had given the Wrangler to Lisa as an anniversary present a few months before she died, purchasing it from one of the dealerships his brother-in-law, Mason Xavier, owned, and back then it had been bright yellow, Lisa's favorite color. Following her murder, Mike had blackened the Jeep, partly as part of his mourning process, but mostly just because it better matched his somber mood. His cowardice, his failure as a man, as a husband, had left him with little use for light or color in his life.

Once settled in the driver's seat, Mike closed the door and started the engine to get the A/C going. Next, he swiveled his head three hundred and sixty degrees, then checked and double-checked his mirrors. Satisfied there were no witnesses to his imminent transgression, he leaned over and retrieved a flask from the glove box.

Really? some inner voice chided. *Right here in the church parking lot?*

That voice was always chastising him, but he had learned how to ignore it. Or rather, how to drown it.

He uncapped the flask and took a slug, grimacing as the bourbon scorched his throat. *Sweet liquid fire,* he thought, twisting the cap back on and tossing the flask back in the glove compartment. He swiped his mouth with the back of his hand and shifted the Jeep into gear.

As he swung the Wrangler out of its parking spot, the cross on the crest of the church steeple blocked the sun and splayed a cruciform shadow across the hood of the vehicle. From Mike's vantage point, looking through the windshield, the cross appeared upside down. Gooseflesh abruptly infested his arms, and he gunned the engine, spitting gravel from his tires, suddenly desperate to be away from this place. As he headed down Route 3 toward Whisper Falls, he felt chilled to the bone despite the booze burning in his guts.

SEVEN

IT WAS a short drive to town. By the time Mike stopped at the intersection by the Chinese restaurant that featured the best General Tso's chicken in the Adirondacks—and the worst fried rice—the internal chill had pretty much faded away and been replaced by a faint sense of hope. It was an unfamiliar sensation, one he had not felt in years. But tomorrow, he would have got his son back and had a plan in place to at least start the reconnection process. Would it be easy? Hell, no. He suffered no delusions that it would be. But it had to be better than the drink-sleep-repeat pattern that had been his existence these last few years.

He took a left onto Main Street and found a parking spot near the town hall. This being the weekend, parking was easy to find—during the work week, you had a better chance of finding naked pictures of the pope canoodling with nuns on Instagram than you did finding a spot in the village's primary parking lots. For being a fairly small, quaint mountain town, Whisper Falls was busier than most people expected. In the summer, they came to the area for the abundance of sparkling lakes and mountain climbing, while in the fall, they came to leaf-peep the spectacular foliage, and in the winter, the ski resorts and snowmobile trails brought in the crowds. About the only season the region was mostly barren of tourists was early spring, when everything turned to mud after the deep winter snow had melted.

He locked the Jeep and strolled up the sidewalk, passing a variety of shops and businesses, offering a polite wave every now and then when he saw someone he knew. He spotted Wanda, the bank manager who had helped him and Lisa set up their accounts when they first moved to the area, coming out of the furniture store. On the other side of street, the owner of the local music emporium was outside washing his storefront window.

Further up was another Chinese restaurant—this one with the best fried rice—just a few doors down from the taxidermy shop that had closed last year after Stone—in his sheriff role—had been forced to shoot the owner when the guy pulled a gun on him rather than go down for a murder charge.

Mike passed the department store outlet, novelty shops, insurance agencies, a tattoo parlor, and the Jack Lumber Bar & Grill. He made a mental note to stop by after his errand and grab a smashburger to go. Maybe down a beer or three while he waited for the food to cook.

After a short walk, he arrived at his destination: Ruff Rick's Sporting Goods and Pet Supplies. It had always seemed like an odd combination, but Rick seemed to make it work, and a lot of people stopped in to buy a box of bullets and a bag of dog food at the same time. The sign dangling from rusty chains above the sidewalk was weather-worn, and several letters were missing, so the sign actually read: *R FF RI K'S S ORTI G GO DS AN PET*

SUP LI S. It looked like a giant cryptogram or a puzzle on Wheel of Fortune.

When Mike walked into Rick's, the first thing he noticed was all the guns—row after row of rifles, shotguns, pistols, and even archery equipment and other assorted hunting gear. The place had been here forever and suffered a reputation as being a bit of a hole in the wall, but the locals chalked it up to being part of the charm, and there was no denying it was well-stocked. Besides, it was the only game in town unless you felt like driving over to Saranac Lake. Mike preferred to support local vendors whenever he could. Besides, there was just something appealing about Ruff Rick's. He felt like a kid in a candy shop whenever he walked in.

More like an alcoholic at a Jim Beam distillery.

Mike ignored the nasty, sneering voice in his head as the owner appeared from a back room, sweeping aside a beaded curtain. Rick was an average-sized man, but he seemed to possess a wiry strength—you could actually see cords of lean muscle hard and rigid beneath his skin. He had one of those faces that didn't forecast his age, making it impossible to judge if he was closer to fifty or eighty.

"Hey, Mike, how's it hangin'? Wait, don't tell me—down an' to the left." Rick grinned crookedly. It was the same jokey greeting he used on Mike every time he came into the store. Personally, Mike thought it was getting a little stale after all these years, and some new material was in order, but Rick apparently disagreed. "So, what brings you down to my humble little rat-hole on a Sunday afternoon?"

"Need a new gun," Mike said.

"Well, son, you've come to the right place." Rick gestured around the store. "Rifles, shotguns, handguns, muzzle loaders—hell, I've even got some crossbows and I think I might have a genuine flamethrower tucked away in the back. So, what exactly are ya lookin' for?"

"I don't know...what do you suggest?"

"I suggest wipin' your ass front to back before askin' a gal to lick your balls."

Mike blinked at him, not exactly sure what to say to that. "Um, what do you suggest for a gun, I meant."

"Oh. My bad." Rick's eyes twinkled merrily, clearly amused by his own unique brand of humor. "Well, that depends on what kind of huntin' you're doin'."

"Small game, mostly. Varmints. That kind of thing."

"What kind of country we talkin' about? What's the terrain like?"

"Going up to Scar Lake."

"Scar Lake, huh?" Rick suddenly looked pensive, his brow furrowing in thought. "Well, lemme tell ya, son, Scar Lake ain't exactly the friendliest place the Good Lord ever spoke into existence. Lots of big-ass rocks and bad-ass bush and bitch-ass thorns. In other words, some real nasty shit up in those parts. Most any shot you get is gonna be up close an' personal, probably less than fifty yards, would be my guess, so ya really don't need a high-power rifle. Shotgun would work best in that area, I think, and I've got just the thing."

He turned, grabbed a shotgun off the rack behind him, and handed it to Mike while rattling off the particulars. "Stoeger Model 2000, semi-automatic, twelve-gauge, synthetic stock, rifled slug barrel. Shorter than a lot of other shotguns and weighs less than seven pounds. Perfect for crawling around in that nasty bush up around Scar Lake."

Mike had to admit that it sounded like just what he was in the market for. He hefted it in his hands and tried to catch a discreet peek at the price tag dangling from a string tied to the trigger guard. But no matter which way he turned the gun, the little white tag twisted away from him. After several seconds, he gave up trying to be discreet and just clumsily grabbed the tag to hold it still. He studied the price and then raised an eyebrow at Rick. "Are you serious?"

"I can sell you a more expensive one if ya want," Rick said with a grin that displayed strong, sturdy teeth stacked in his gums like tombstones.

"No, no, this is good. Thanks."

Rick chuckled. "Thought you'd say that." They moved over to the cash register tucked into the corner of the cramped store. A loosely stacked pyramid of canned cat food looked like it was about to tip over. Mike handed over his credit card and listened to Rick whistle tunelessly while waiting for the receipt to print. A few moments later, Rick handed him the receipt along with a complimentary box of shells for the shotgun and a final warning: "Be careful up there. Scar Lake is dangerous country if ya let down your guard. Hate to get one of those missin' person alerts about you on my phone."

"Not sure there's anyone around who would actually miss me." Mike pocketed the receipt, slung the gun over his shoulder, and added, "But don't worry, careful is my middle name."

"Yeah, well, mine's Cornelius." Rick gave him a faux menacing glare. "Tell anyone and I swear they'll never find your fuckin' corpse."

EIGHT

THE CRACK of gunfire split the afternoon heat. The Smith & Wesson Stealth Hunter Performance .44 Magnum revolver bucked in Stone's right fist. His left hand fastened a tight grip on Rocky's reins as the appaloosa stallion thundered through the woods like a medieval steed charging into battle.

The target flew backward, drilled through the chest by the heavy bullet, and slumped into the underbrush.

Stone thudded his bootheels into the horse's flanks, urging the appaloosa to even greater speeds as he spotted another threat, little more than a dangerous shadow, lurking between a pair of white birch trees. Hidden, but not enough to escape Stone's sharp eyes. Rocky surged forward, muscles coiled like springs as his hooves punched into the pine needle-covered dirt, churning up soil and flinging clods in his wake.

Stone thumbed back the hammer and stroked the trigger. The Smith & Wesson roared again, slamming a bullet into the figure between the trees, dead on target. The head snapped backward, its contents exploding from the gaping exit hole.

Stone usually found peace, solace, and comfort in riding Rocky over the trails in the thick woods behind his house, but not this afternoon. Today, hostiles lurked in the trees and Stone needed to deal with them—fast, hard, and without mercy. Less than a year ago, a ragtag militia recruited by an escaped convict—Holly's ex-husband and Lizzy's father—had stormed through these very same woods, looking to put him down and reap the reward promised by the murderous mob boss. Stone had put bullets into each and every one of them.

Just like he was going to do now.

Sunlight filtered down through the tree branches in fragmented streaks as Rocky barreled nimbly through the woods, moving as fast as the tight conditions allowed. This wasn't the stallion's first time dealing with threats, and he performed with skill and confidence. Stone's eyes scanned the terrain, seeking out any other would-be assailants lying in wait for him.

There, thirty yards away, he spotted a third gunman, crouched low, weapon drawn and aimed. The gunner hesitated on the shot, as if paralyzed by the sight of Stone powering toward him on a galloping horse with a hand-cannon in his fist.

Stone made him pay for his inaction. The .44 Magnum bucked, and the man's right eye disappeared, leaving behind a ragged hole that went all the way through his head.

Rocky kept moving, hurdling over a fallen log with a graceful leap. As soon as the stallion touched down, Stone glimpsed another threat on his left peripheral. He twisted in the saddle and triggered a shot, putting the bullet right in the target's mouth.

Stone hauled back on the reins and brought the horse to a halt, the appaloosa happy to comply. The Smith &

Wesson revolver returned to its leather shoulder rig, then Stone removed his Stetson and sleeved sweat from his brow before settling the cowboy hat back in place.

Without the noise of gunfire and pounding hooves, the woods seemed quiet and still. Off in the distance, a crow cawed, as if protesting all the chaos and commotion. Rocky shook his head and sent his mane flying to ward off some annoying flies that seemed intent on settling on horseflesh. In prime shape, the stallion wasn't breathing that hard, but he would definitely need some water when they got back to the barn, along with a good rubdown.

Stone turned around in the saddle to look behind him at the targets. Two of them were *scarecrows*—burlap sacks stuffed with straw—and the other two were full-size paper targets with threatening gunmen printed on them. He sometimes rigged them up in the woods for training purposes. Today, he needed a distraction, a way to let off some steam.

Holly still wasn't answering his calls or responding to his texts. He knew it had been less than forty-eight hours, but he still felt irritable about it. Worse, he felt hollow and hurting, an emotional pain that pressed against his heart like a hot iron.

Damn it, Theresa, why did you have to get drunk and leave that stupid message?

After retrieving the cabin key from Pastor Burke and delivering it to Mike Donner, he had decided to take his mind off things by running through a tactical training session. Because what kind of *cowboy preacher* would he be if he didn't know how to shoot a gun while riding a horse? Besides, he knew better than most that it paid to keep your warrior skills sharp.

But none of it had worked to take his mind off Holly.

Rocky pawed at the ground as if sensing his rider's

troubled spirit. Stone leaned over and patted the horse's neck, then ran a hand over the bristly mane. "You're right," he muttered to the stallion. "She'll call when she's ready."

He almost believed it.

NINE

A BLINDING, relentless light pulled Mike Donner from his slumbering stupor and a dream—no, nightmare—in which he was making love to Lisa, only to find at the peak of their passion that she turned into a decomposing corpse beneath him, crumbling away in chunks of rotting flesh and powdery bones. The horrific mental imagery dissipated when he cracked open his eyes and then immediately winced as they were lanced by the sunlight stabbing through his bedroom window.

He sat up and clutched his pounding head, which was brutally hammering home the fact that he had drunk way too much last night. No surprise there—he had drunk too much almost every night since he lost Lisa. One of his relatives had once asked him if he was seeing a therapist to deal with his grief. He had told them that he was seeing three of them, and their names were Jim Beam, Jack Daniels, and Wild Turkey. His relative had chuckled at the joke, not realizing Mike wasn't joking.

His stomach suddenly revolted. He bolted from his bed and stumbled into the bathroom, barely having time to lift the lid before he heaved into the toilet. He slumped to his knees, a drunkard sinner kneeling before his porcelain god, and spent several wrenching moments paying penance in vomit. Cold sweat beaded his brow, and for a brief moment, he thought it was over.

He thought wrong.

"Oh, crap," he managed to mumble just before his guts rebelled again, forcing him to remain huddled over the bowl. His knees started to hurt. He was going to need some ibuprofen to chase away the ache. After spending so many mornings in this position, you would think he would have learned to put a mat in front of the toilet.

When he finished, he managed to pull himself upright and lurched over to the sink, where he washed his mouth out with Listerine—the alcoholic's friend—and splashed cold water on his face. When he looked into the mirror, his red eyes stared back and accused him of self-destruction. It was an accusation that he couldn't deny. *What the hell is wrong with me?* He rubbed a hand over his bleary features and muttered, "My god, man, you are not a pretty sight." Probably the understatement of the year.

No longer wanting to face his own degeneration in the mirror, he turned to look at the clock radio perched on a nearby shelf. The large numbers were even redder than his eyes and informed him it was 10:42 a.m. It took him a few foggy seconds to realize why that was important, but then his brain kicked into gear. Something close to panic hit him. "Great! Just fucking great. Of all the times to tie one on." He continued to silently berate himself. *Stupid! You're so damn stupid, Mike.*

He needed a shower, but there was no time. He quickly changed his clothes, brushed his teeth, ran a comb through his hair, and then sprinted to the Jeep like a dumbass son of a bitch who had just screwed up royally.

At Brighton Juvenile Detention Center, Carson Donner slouched on a bench outside the main building. After three years behind the fence, it felt strange being free. The *nice* thing about prison was that you didn't have to think much for yourself. The officers pretty much told you when to eat, when to sleep, when to work, when to relax...hell, they practically told you when to do everything except take a piss, shit, and jerk off. Those particular activities were left up to your own discretion.

He could clearly remember the day he had been brought to the detention center, bused there along with a handful of other so-called delinquents. Guilty of various crimes—his happened to be robbing Sloane's Emporium, the closest thing Whisper Falls had to a Walmart—they had all felt like tough guys. But in hindsight, they had been nothing but naïve children. Being behind bars forced you to grow up fast, and the meat grinder of the justice system turned soft boys into hard men. It had not been pleasant, but now that it was over, Carson was thankful for the hardening.

Still, he wasn't looking forward to what came next. He had missed many things while locked up, but his father wasn't one of them. He idly wondered what sort of pathetic attempt at reconciliation his old man had in store.

He ran his fingers, knuckles calloused from numerous brawls on the recreation yard, through what little hair still tufted his head—they gave all the juvies a jailbird haircut—and idly wondered what he would look like if he grew it down to his shoulders like some '80s hair-metal rock star. Maybe he would buy a bandana and enter a Bret Michaels lookalike contest. He could croon a pretty decent rendition of "Every Rose Has Its Thorns."

Thoughts of rock 'n' roll fakery dissipated as the piercing squeal of tires protesting their punishment announced his father's arrival. Mike took the corner way too fast, nearly rolling the Wrangler, and screeched to a halt in front of Carson. A cloud of road dust drifted in the Jeep's wake.

Mike glanced at the dashboard clock—11:06 a.m. Okay, he was late, but not by much. He rolled down the window, gave Carson a smile, and said, "Ready to go?" It was a stupid question—after three years in prison, of course he was ready to go—but Mike didn't know what else to say. He hadn't spoken to his son in thirty-six months, so it was almost like talking to a stranger. Conversation was bound to be awkward from time to time. Maybe all the time.

Carson just sat, posture slouched, and glared at his father for several long moments, the distaste on his face impossible to misread. Then he straightened up, stretched, grabbed a small duffel bag, and ambled his way over to the Jeep. Mike was struck by how much the boy had grown. Even beneath a loose-fitting t-shirt, it was pretty obvious that his son was now a well-muscled young man. Before Carson had been sentenced to juvenile detention, Mike would have easily beaten him in a fight. Now the outcome wouldn't be so easy to predict.

But it wasn't a physical confrontation Carson seemed to want—it was a verbal one.

His son climbed into the Wrangler and slammed the door much harder than was necessary. Wasting no time on false pleasantries, Carson growled, "You're late."

Even his voice is deeper, Mike thought, as he whipped the Jeep around and shot back out onto Route 86. The tension he felt translated to his foot, which stomped heavy on the gas pedal. When he realized the needle was pegged at a point on the speedometer that no self-respecting police officer would find acceptable, Mike eased off and forced himself to slow down. Judging from Carson's sullen tone, this was about to turn into a bad day, and catching a speeding ticket would only make it worse.

Traffic fines mean less money for whiskey, right?

Mike ignored the inner taunt and kept his voice neutral as he said, "Nice to see you, too, Carson. And I was barely late. I overslept."

"In what, a barrel of booze?" Carson sneered. "You smell like you just got done with a three-day bender and forgot to shower. Just how hard are you hitting the bottle these days, *Dad*?"

Mike resisted the urge to turn and glare at him. Instead, he kept his eyes firmly fixed on the road. "I don't *hit the bottle,* Carson. I have a social drink now and then, that's it." The lie slipped smooth and easy off his tongue.

But he could tell his son wasn't buying the deception. Carson's stare burned a hole in the side of his head. When another quarter mile had rolled beneath the Jeep's knobby tires, Carson suddenly reached for the glove box.

"No!" Mike said, throwing out an arm to stop him.

Too late. Carson held up the flask like a prosecutor triumphantly revealing a damning piece of evidence. "Yeah, pops," he drawled sarcastically, "because every social drinker keeps a flask in the glove compartment." He shook his head in disgust.

So much for keeping it neutral, Mike thought. Aloud, he said, "I'm your father, and I don't have to explain myself to you." He hated how defensive the words sounded even to his own ears.

Carson was silent for several moments, then said,

"You're right, you don't have to explain anything." For a moment, Mike actually dared to hope Carson was calling a truce, but then his son added, "I'd probably drink myself stupid too if I'd killed my wife because I was a goddamned coward."

The words were designed to hurt…and hurt they did. Horribly. Mike would have preferred Carson to just whip out a knife and start slashing him to ribbons. It would have been less painful.

He was quiet for several miles, distracting his pain by listening to the sounds of the road, the thrum of the tires on blacktop, the rush of the wind, a bluesy Aerosmith rocker crooning low-volume on the radio. Despite Carson's presence just an arm's reach away, he felt isolated and alone. As he had, ever since that dark day a madman showed up at his door and murdered his wife while Mike sat there like a gutless coward.

Up ahead, a road sign appeared that read Welcome to Whisper Falls. As they drove by it and started weaving their way through town, Mike said, "I've made peace with what happened to your mother."

Carson shook the flask. The booze sloshing around inside sounded like the devil's accusation. "Yeah, I can see that you're really at peace." Scorn roughened his voice.

Mike didn't say anything as he drove through town, but when he reached the outskirts, he kept his left hand on the steering wheel and snatched the flask out of Carson's hand with his right.

"Hey, what the hell?" Carson protested.

Mike rolled down his window and threw out the flask. Glancing in his rearview mirror, he saw it tumble along the shoulder and drop out of sight over a bank that led down to the Saranac River. Some trout fisherman would probably find it.

"Really?" Carson said. "What was that all about?"

"Something I should have done a long time ago. I'm done drinking," Mike announced. He tried to ignore the panic curdling his guts at the sobering thought of having to spend several days in the woods with his bitter, angry, standoffish son without any alcohol to help him get through.

"Just like that, huh?" Carson asked.

"Yeah, just like that."

Carson's laugh was tauntingly sarcastic. "I call bull-shit…but whatever. Now, care to tell me where we're going? Because it's clearly not home."

Grateful for the change in subject, Mike said, "Scar Lake."

"For what?"

"To get away. Do a little varmint hunting. Thought you might like to chill out and relax a bit before getting back to the daily grind."

"Any strippers? I've been locked up and haven't seen a girl for three years, other than prison staff, and they don't count." Carson grinned. "I could definitely go for some *relaxing*, if you know what I mean."

Mike shot him a wry glance. "It's hunting camp, not a brothel."

"Hunting camp." Carson shook his head. "What a stupid idea. In case your observational skills have been compromised by that supposedly final bender you went on last night, the only clothes I have with me are the ones I'm wearing. So, if you want to go traipsing through the ass end of God's backyard, I'm going to need more appropriate attire." His voice dripped with sarcasm as he added, "Oh yeah, and a gun."

Mike jerked a thumb toward the rear of the Jeep. "I packed you a bag," he said. "And that long box back there is for you."

Carson glanced over his shoulder. "What's in it?"

"Best way to find that out is to open it."

Carson reached behind him and pulled the box into the front seat. The length made it awkward, but he managed, only knocking Mike in the head once, and probably on purpose. He opened the box to find the Stoeger shotgun nestled inside in a cradle of Styrofoam. The heady scents of gunmetal and cleaning oil filled the Jeep with their testosteronic aroma.

"Got it from Ruff Rick's," Mike said. "Brand new, never been shot, ready for action."

He hoped his son's abrasive, resentful shell would crack, at least a little bit, but no such luck. "A Stoeger?" Carson said mockingly. "Isn't that like the Walmart of shotguns? What's the matter, Dad, spend too much money on booze so you couldn't afford a real gun like a Mossberg or Remington?"

Mike didn't respond. Just gripped the steering wheel a little harder.

Carson's tone abruptly shifted from mocking to venomous. "I can see right through your little plan, *Dad*." He sneered the endearment so that it sounded like a twisted obscenity. "You thought giving me this shotgun would patch things up between us, make things all right, bridge the gap, heal the wound, that sort of crap." The lines on his face were rigid, the muscles tight and tense. "But let me tell you something, it's gonna take a whole lot more than a new gun and some *bond in nature* time to make me forgive you for what you did to Mom."

The words were cold daggers, each one stabbing deep into Mike's heart. He turned his head to the left, not wanting Carson to see his eyes welling up. Shame and anger seesawed through him at the same time, and he blinked back tears as he white-knuckled the wheel and struggled to regain control of his wavering emotions.

When he could speak again, Mike said, "I know I failed you, Carson. I failed all of us. Your mom most of all. But I'm not the same person I was back then." He had a hard time forcing the words out around the lump in his throat.

"Right," said Carson. "Before, you were just a coward. Now you're a coward and a drunk. I guess that's evolution." He snorted dismissively. "Save your words, Dad. They're just as cheap as this shotgun you bought me." He tossed the Stoeger into the back of the Jeep.

Mike could take no more and lapsed into silence, keeping his eyes on the road as his embers of hope for a fresh start with his son were extinguished by Carson's cold anger. Not that he could blame him. Carson had every right to hate his father. Hell, he hated himself most of the time.

Mike glanced at his reflection in the rearview mirror. His face looked older, more wrinkled, than it had an hour ago, and sadness veiled his eyes. He struggled to fight back the internal darkness that wanted to descend. He could not give in. He *would not* give in. He would never give up on his son.

But refusing to acknowledge defeat and knowing what to say to achieve victory were two different things, so the embargo of silence remained firmly in place. Carson refused to give an inch, and Mike felt like he had no more inches to give. Not right now, anyway.

They stopped at the convenience store in Redford to grab some snacks—Mike lingered longingly in front of the beer cooler, the ice-cold sixpacks calling his name like a siren's song—but managed to pull himself away before continuing down the highway, each of them chewing on a beef stick and pointedly not talking to each other.

They eventually turned off State Route 3 onto side roads that devolved into gravel roads that devolved into dirt roads. Finally, over two hours after leaving the Brighton Juvenile Detention Center, Mike pulled the Jeep into a small parking turnoff and shut off the engine. There was only one other vehicle parked nearby, a Ford Escape with New Jersey license plates and a sticker on the rear window that proclaimed: ***MEAT IS MURDER***, in thick, bold letters.

Mike shook his head. "Vegans. I'll bet you ten bucks they're wearing leather boots while they hike." They were the first words he had spoken in over an hour and a half.

He took the key out of the ignition and exited the Wrangler. He arched his back and stretched to relieve the aches of the road, muscles murmuring in relief. Breathing in the mountain air, he felt his spirits start to revive, pushing back some of the melancholic darkness that had settled over him. He hoped the beautifully rugged surroundings were having a similar effect on Carson. He turned and looked at his son as he climbed out of the Jeep.

Carson slowly and deliberately made a point of looking in all directions, not missing a single compass point, and then said, "I don't see any cabin."

Mike walked to the back of the vehicle and began grabbing their gear. "Gotta hike our way back. About three miles, give or take."

"Three miles!" Carson sounded as if he had just been told they were walking to Budapest. "Are you kidding me?"

Grinning, Mike tossed him a pack. "I kid you not."

Carson did not look amused as he slipped his arms through the pack's shoulder straps. "Should've just stayed in juvie," he muttered.

Mike walked over to the trail register, a small wooden shack next to a large pine tree at the head of the trail. As he jotted their names down on the ledger, he saw the only other two names listed were Sonya and Ted Sawyer, presumably the same people who equated eating a hamburger to homicide.

As he shifted his pack to better distribute the weight, Carson looked at the Ford Escape's out-of-state tags and shook his head. "What kind of clowns drive all the way from New Jersey to come to this godforsaken back-country?"

"I don't know if they're clowns, but their names are Sonya and Ted Sawyer," said Mike.

"Clowns or not, they should have stuck to safer turf," Carson said. "This far back in the butt-crack of nowhere, there are at least fifty ways to die, and none of them are pleasant."

Mike shrugged. "Hey, they live in New Jersey, so how smart can they be? Come on, let's get moving."

They followed a narrow trail through the thick forest of pine, maple, birch, and oak. The afternoon sun speared through the foliage in golden shafts, reflecting off the leaves. Mike appreciated the organic beauty, Mother Nature painting on the canvas God created.

A couple hundred yards up the path, they came to a gulch spanned by a makeshift rope-and-log bridge that looked like it might have been constructed right around the end of the Civil War. Mike debated just going down into the gulch, but the sides were steep, and jagged boulders protruded from the earthen walls like the discarded teeth of some giant monster. It was just too dangerous.

So is that bridge, his inner voice cautioned.

But there really wasn't much choice. They either took their chances with the rickety bridge or they turned back, and turning back wasn't an option for Mike. Besides, Sonya and Ted Sawyer had obviously made it across. If they had fallen, their busted-up bodies would be lying at the bottom of the ravine in a pile of snapped limbs and broken bones.

Taking a deep breath—*For once in your life, don't be a pathetic coward,* he said to himself—Mike put one tentative foot in front of the other and gingerly crossed the bridge. It felt like it took forever. He only looked down once, and seeing the trout stream snaking along the bottom of the gulch far below in liquid-silver flashes made the world spin, and he grabbed the thick rope that substituted as a handrail in order to regain his equilibrium. Then he fixed his eyes on the opposite side and finished crossing as quickly as he could, trying to ignore the hammering of his heart. He breathed an audible sigh of relief when his feet touched solid ground again.

He watched anxiously as Carson trekked across the bridge, but his son seemed to take it all in stride. He even looked down through the gaps in the logs most of the time and showed no signs of vertigo.

That's my boy, Mike thought. *One tough kid.* Aloud, he said, "Pretty nerve-racking, huh?"

Carson brushed past him with a curt reply. "Only if you're a pussy." After another hundred yards or so, he headed into the thick brush alongside the trail. "Be right back. Gotta take a piss."

As he waited for Carson to answer the call of nature, Mike noticed a pine tree just off the trail with a trunk that forked into a perfect *Y* about twenty feet up. A vine-covered log had fallen into the crotch and was perfectly balanced, the forked tree acting as the fulcrum to form a giant teeter-totter. The log was angled down, one end disappearing into the thicket while the other end jutted upward at a forty-five-degree angle over the trail.

"Hey," Mike called to Carson. "Hurry up, will you? We're burning daylight."

"Don't rush me," Carson said from the bushes.

A salamander caught Mike's eye, scurrying along the trail. He almost missed it, the little lizard's brown and black coloration the perfect camouflage to blend into the dirt and leaves. Mike stepped forward and leaned over for a closer look.

The end of the teeter-totter log that had been jutting out over the trail suddenly dropped down like an executioner's axe, smashing the ground just inches in front of his face and crushing the salamander into amphibious pulp. Mike jumped back so quickly that he tripped and landed on his back. His pack cushioned the fall but left him sprawled in the middle of the trail like a turned-over turtle.

Carson peered at him from behind a thorn bush.

Mike rolled onto his knees and yelled, "You almost killed me!"

Carson at least had the courtesy to look a little sheepish. "Uh, yeah," he said. "My bad."

Mike climbed to his feet and dusted off his pants while glaring at his son. "You nearly busted my head with a humongous log, and all you can say is *my bad*?"

Carson reached up and pulled on a vine dangling from the log. The rope-like vegetation was as thick as his forearm. He pulled on it, and his end of the log swung down while the opposite end rose back into the air, dripping salamander guts, until it was once again angled above the trail. He then pushed through the brush and rejoined his father on the path.

"Could always be worse," he said, taking the lead as they resumed their hike.

"Yeah? How so?" Mike asked.

Carson looked back over his shoulder and replied, "I could've said, 'Shit, I missed.'"

Mike frowned at him. "You're not funny."

"Have a drink," Carson shot back. "Maybe you'll find me more amusing."

A defensive response quickly rose to Mike's lips, but at the last second, he decided to let it go. It just wasn't worth it, and nothing he said would change Carson's mind.

They hiked in silence until they came to a sharp bend that led up into a pine grove that was thick with shadows, the sun barely penetrating the twisted, interlocked canopy of needle-laden branches overhead. Mike abruptly halted.

"Why are you stopping?" Carson asked.

"I think this is where that girl, Pastor Burke's daughter, got killed."

"Read about that in the paper," Carson said. "Bear got her, right?"

Mike nodded. "Ripped her apart before her father could do anything about it. Not that there was much he could have done."

"That had to suck."

"Watching someone you love get killed right before your eyes? Yeah, that kind of sucks big time."

Carson stared at him with hooded, piercing eyes. Mike held his gaze for just the briefest of moments and then looked away. He started walking again, and even though he didn't really believe in ghosts, he still felt a little strange traipsing over ground where someone had died. Pastor Stone or Sheriff Stone or whatever you called him, had cautioned about the dangers of the area when he had met up with Mike to give him the key to the cabin, and the tragic tale of Jenny Burke's death had been one of the examples he used to make his point.

As they walked, Mike finished telling the story to Carson. "I guess her father went right at the bear with just his walking stick and got hurt pretty bad for it. He had to leave Jenny's body behind and go for help. Hurt like he was, it took him almost a whole day—you saw how far we are from the nearest town. By the time anyone got back here, the bear was long gone, and all that was left of his daughter was a lot of blood and one finger that had been bitten off. It still had her class ring on it." He paused for a moment and shook his head. "I can't even imagine."

"Sure, you can," said Carson.

Now it was Mike's turn to fire off a piercing glare.

Carson raised his hands in mock surrender. "Hey, I'm just saying."

"How about instead of trying to pick a fight, you pick up the pace," Mike replied. "I'd like to be at the cabin before dark if that's okay with you."

With that, an unspoken truce seemed to be reached, and they hiked the remaining miles without saying another word to each other. By focusing on their pace instead of their hostility, they managed to arrive at the cabin with plenty of daylight to spare. Mike breathed a sigh of relief as the building appeared through the trees. He had not been looking forward to hiking in the dark. The mosquitoes were bad enough in the daytime.

Walking up to the front of the lodge, they stopped and looked it over. If Mike was being honest, the place didn't look like much. Four walls constructed from rough planks, a tarpaper roof with a crooked chimney poking through, and your basic three-step front porch. Calling it a lodge was actually an exercise in wishful thinking. This was a hunter's cabin, pure and simple.

It was obvious that Carson had taken an instant dislike to the rustic accommodations. The disgust was written on his face as he stared at the outhouse with a half-moon carved in the door, squatting about forty yards away from the cabin on the opposite side of the trail, nestled among some saplings.

"This place doesn't even have plumbing?" he asked in disbelief. "Are you kidding me?"

"We're three miles from the nearest road," Mike said, "and that road was ten miles from the nearest town. What did you expect, a Holiday Inn?"

"No, but I didn't expect to play Little House on the Prairie and take a crap outside either."

"People have been doing their business outside since Adam and Eve, so you'll be fine. Let's take a look inside."

A simple clasp and padlock kept things secured. Mike used the key provided by Stone to open the door, and they filed inside to stow their gear. Once the sun went down, he would get a campfire going to roast some hotdogs. He'd even brought Carson's favorite kind, the ones filled with cheese.

Just the thought of sitting outside by a crackling fire while eating a frankfurter, watching the sparks spiral up into the dark like fireflies, made him crave a cold beer. He was glad he hadn't brought any. He wasn't sure he could have resisted the urge, and since Carson already considered him a failure, breaking his promise to stop drinking would have just further nailed that belief in place.

As they entered the cabin, neither of them happened to glance toward the outhouse, but even if they had, it was unlikely they would have spotted the one-eyed man concealed in the thick brush behind the wooden latrine. Patch remained silent and still, conditioned for the hunt. He didn't even move when a deerfly landed on his eyepatch.

He watched for several more minutes, mouth curled in a cruel, satisfied smile, and then skulked away to tell the others about the new prey that had just shown up.

Fresh meat, hell yeah.

TEN

STONE WASN'T in the best of moods by the time Monday evening rolled around. Still nothing from Holly. He understood she was hurt and upset, but ignoring him for three days seemed unreasonable, and frankly, unjustified. He was a direct approach kind of guy and hated just leaving a problem hanging out there unresolved, especially when it would only be fixed by talking things out. In his mind, silence didn't help anything. But apparently, Holly disagreed with his assessment and right now the ball was in her court.

It had also been a busy day at the office. No major crimes, but a bunch of petty stuff that had to be dealt with. Vandals kicking over gravestones at the cemetery, a shoplifter at the gas station, a shoving match at McDonald's because the flurry machine was broken for the fifth day in a row, a drunk and disorderly call—before noon, no less—at one of the less savory motels in town. All relatively easy to handle, but it meant the paperwork piled up, and paperwork never did anything to improve his mood.

He was just getting ready to call it a day and head

over to the Jack Lumber for a post-shift drink when Deputy Cade Valentine stepped into the office. "You got a minute, sheriff?"

Stone sized up the young man standing in front of him. At only twenty-seven, Valentine was the rookie on the force, but he had several years of service behind him, so you couldn't actually call him wet behind the ears anymore. Plus, he'd taken bullets in the line of duty, having been ambushed by neo-Nazis a couple of years back. The guy had grit, no doubt about it. But right now, he sounded nervous.

"Sure," Stone said. "Come on in, take a load off, tell me what's on your mind. Unless you'd rather head over to the bar and talk there."

Valentine shook his head. "No, I'd rather just go ahead and get this over with."

Stone leaned back in his chair. "Well, that sounds ominous."

"Not sure you're gonna like what I have to say."

"Doesn't mean you shouldn't say it."

Valentine closed the door behind him and sat down in one of the chairs facing Stone's paperwork-strewn desk. He didn't speak, the silence settling uneasy between them. Stone waited him out, perfectly comfortable with uncomfortable silences. The young deputy clearly had something on his mind, but he would spit it out when he was good and ready. Stone saw no reason to rush him. It wasn't like Holly was waiting for him or anything.

Valentine reached up and ran his fingers through his red hair, took a deep breath like a man steadying himself for a dive into deep waters, and finally spoke. "First off, sir, I want you to know that I respect you. Not just a little, but a whole hell of a lot. I want to get that out in the open right from the get-go."

"Fair enough," Stone said. "It's out in the open, and I appreciate you saying so."

"I mean it," Valentine continued. "You've done a lot of good things since you took over after Sheriff Camden, that rotten bastard. Hell, you weren't even the sheriff yet when you took down that child trafficking ring. Then you busted up a meth ring, defended this place against those neo-Nazi pricks, took down an escaped convict, and even rescued some missionaries last month."

Stone gave him an apprising look. "Cade, mind telling me why you're rattling off a list of my accomplishments?"

Valentine squared his shoulders. "Because I want you to know that I think you've done a lot of good things for the people in Garrison County."

"I'm getting the impression there's a *but* coming."

"But I think the people deserve a sheriff who doesn't play so fast and loose with the rules." The words came out in a rush, and Valentine sighed heavily after saying them, as if relieved to finally have them out in the open.

Stone remained still, studying the young deputy. "You got a problem with how I wear the badge?"

"Honestly? Yeah, sometimes. You have to admit, sir, that de-escalation is not one of your strengths. You're pretty quick to go to guns to resolve problems."

"I believe in justice, Cade."

"I believe in justice, too," Valentine said. "I also believe in the law."

"Those aren't always the same thing. In fact, sometimes the law gets in the way of justice."

"No offense, sir, but I didn't come here to debate with you."

"No, I reckon you didn't," Stone said. "My guess is that you came here to tell me you're throwing your hat in the ring and running against me for sheriff in the next election."

Valentine nodded. "Like I said, I respect you, and I think you've done good things for this town, but I also think it's time for a change. Little more law and order, a little less cowboy shit."

"It's not like I'm shooting jaywalkers," Stone said. "Anyone I put a bullet in, they had it coming."

"I don't dispute that," Valentine replied. "But you're the kind of guy who seems to think a bullet should be the first option."

"What do you think the first option should be?"

"Arrest, sir. We're cops, not executioners."

Stone sighed. "Listen, Cade, you want my job, you're welcome to try for it."

"It's not personal, sheriff. I promise you that."

"I believe you."

"I just think I can offer the town something it needs." Valentine's voice had steadied during the course of the conversation, the nervousness at the beginning replaced by the strength of his beliefs. "More suspects behind bars instead of buried in boot-hill."

Stone felt the weight of the words, felt the conviction behind them. Hell, he had wrestled—sometimes *still* wrestled—with his killing ways for years, so it was no surprise to hear someone else questioning the fact that he was quick on the trigger. He understood where Valentine was coming from, even if he didn't fully agree.

The deputy was still talking. "I know some people like your cowboy brand of law enforcement, like the way you're willing to use blood and thunder to get the job done. But there's a time and a place for everything—isn't that what the Good Book says?—and you just seem to have a knack for finding more times and places to put men in coffins than any other lawman I've ever met."

Stone shrugged. "Maybe God's sending the bastards my way 'cause they need killing and He knows I'll get it done."

"I don't believe justice should always be written in blood."

"That's your problem, Cade. You think justice is always neat and clean." Stone rubbed his bristled jaw wearily. "Some of the world is black and white, I'll give you that. But a lot of it is gray, and a whole lot of justice rides in that gray area."

"You're a damn good man, sheriff," Valentine said. "But you justify killing way too easy."

"You might be right about that," Stone replied, thinking about how his own conscience pricked him sometimes. "But a man can't run from who he is."

"A man can change, and you know it," said Valentine. "If you don't believe that, you've got no business being a preacher, even part-time."

Stone didn't respond. He was too busy thinking that maybe he should just give his badge to Valentine and walk away for good, put his law dog days behind him. He had come to Whisper Falls to be a preacher, to make some kind of feeble atonement for the blood and darkness of his past, not to become the sheriff. He had tried to put his warrior days behind him and failed. But just because you failed at something once didn't mean you couldn't try again. Maybe he should take another shot at putting away his guns and sticking to the pulpit. More preaching, less punishing.

Yeah, food for thought. But he wasn't looking for an easy exit just yet.

He fixed his honey-colored eyes on Valentine. "You said your piece with heart and honesty. I appreciate that. Guess all you can do now is throw your hat in the ring and let the voters decide who they want running things around here."

"No hard feelings?"

"None at all," Stone replied, and he meant it.

"Mind if I ask you something?"

"Fire away."

Valentine shifted in his chair and cleared his throat. "What exactly is your background? You clearly have top-tier government connections to get appointed to this position when Camden died, and your tactical skills suggest some kind of military or spec-ops training. But when I try digging deeper, I come up with a whole bunch of nothing." He leaned forward slightly and locked eyes with Stone. "With all due respect, sir, just who the hell are you?"

Stone returned the deputy's gaze and kept his expression unreadable. "We've all got pasts, Cade. And not all of us care to talk about them."

"My opinion, the people deserve to know the truth about the man wearing the badge in their town."

"You might be right. Doesn't change what I just said."

Valentine nodded, slow and deliberate, like he had just been given a lot to chew on, and then stood up. "Can't force a man to share his secrets, so I guess I'll be on my way. I appreciate you taking the time to see me, sir." He hesitated, as if he had something more to say, but then gave a little shake of his head and walked away.

Stone watched him go and then sat in the chair a long time after he left, reflecting on the blood and shadows and regrets of his warrior days.

God, what do You want from me?

But just like Holly, God seemed to be giving him the silent treatment.

ELEVEN

SITTING IN HER KENNEL-CAGE, the woman looked at the fresh wounds on her arms from where Patch had sliced open her flesh the other night and fought back the despondency that so desperately tried to claim her. It would be easy, so easy, to just give up and surrender to the depths of insanity that clutched at her. She knew there would be peace in letting her mind break—just stop fighting, let her soul tumble until it shattered like an eggshell against the harsh, hopeless reality that was her existence.

But she couldn't do it. That wasn't who she was. She was a fighter, and not even the hell she now endured could change that.

The cuts hurt, but the slashes had scabbed over. More scars to add to the ever-expanding tapestry of pain her body now wore. The wounds would heal, but she would never be the same, physically or mentally. Stuck in a dog cage, tortured by sadistic men, she had been damaged beyond flesh and bone, beyond the marrow, where the deepest depths of the soul dwelled. Even if she somehow, someday, made it out of here alive, she doubted she would ever be able to close her eyes without being transported back to this filthy cabin and cage.

She looked out the window and saw a bloated moon hanging in the heavens. She found solace in the lunar light streaming into her prison, but clouds thickened the night sky, and she knew they would soon snuff out the moonbeams. But that was her life now—slivered moments of peace and respite in the middle of a living hell. She had learned to savor those moments when they came, however brief they might be.

Mr. Joe crouched on the floor of her cage, keeping her company, but seemed distracted by a moth caught in the web over in the corner, powdery wings beating themselves to pieces against the silken strands as the insect struggled to break free. But she spoke to the Joro spider anyway. After all, these conversations were for her benefit, not his. "I don't know how much more I can take, Mr. Joe. It feels like God has left me here to die."

From outside the cabin, a woman's shrill, piercing, horrified scream cut through the night.

The door banged open, and Goliath stomped in. The floorboards thundered and rattled beneath his heavy feet. The spider darted for safety, racing for its web on eight fast-scuttling legs. Goliath dragged a middle-aged woman behind him by the arm, the limb twisted painfully. Her *I Love NJ* shirt was torn, tattered, and smeared with blood.

Honcho entered next, shoving a man in front of him. Rope bound the prisoner's wrists together, and blood caked his face. The man staggered as he was pushed into the cabin, tripping over the threshold and falling to the floor. He looked at the other woman through a mask of red and weakly whispered, "Sonya..."

Sonya screamed, "Ted!" but then Goliath plowed his

fist into her gut so hard that her spleen probably flattened against her spine. The blow literally lifted her off the floor...the floor on which she fell a moment later and curled up in a vomiting ball.

Honcho punched Ted in the face, and teeth exploded from his pulped mouth in a shrapnel-like spray of shattered enamel. A second blow splattered Ted's nose from cheek to cheek and rendered him unconscious. Honcho then flung the man into the corner like unwanted trash before directing his attention to Sonya.

The woman in the cage turned her head away as Sonya was yanked off the floor and slammed down on the table. She didn't want to witness the ugly brutality that happened next.

The abuse.

The violation.

The cutting.

The blood.

She closed her eyes as Sonya screamed and shrieked and pleaded, her voice filling the cabin with the sound of hopeless despair as the men took turns doing whatever they wanted to her.

When it was over, Honcho walked over to the kennel, his face streaked with sweat. The woman hurriedly retreated to the rear as he opened the padlock.. Goliath unceremoniously dumped Sonya into the cage—they weren't done with her, not by a long shot, not until they had harvested her organs—and Honcho locked it back up.

The two women stared at each other. One with eyes sad and haunted from endless months in hell, and one with eyes bewildered and terrified because her hell had just begun. Sonya's body, her clothes now nothing but torn strips, bore the signs of brutalization. Her arms and legs were covered with slashes, blood weeping from the wounds. The woman knew something that Sonya didn't —one day soon, those wounds would deepen, the blades digging deeper until she was dead, her flesh sliced away and sold in the name of greed and profit.

Up in the corner, Mr. Joe slowly stalked over to the moth entangled in the web. The insect's frantic struggles had considerably weakened, and the spider hovered over its prey, patiently waiting for just the right moment to strike.

Goliath slapped Ted into consciousness and then jerked him to his feet. The New Jersey native was a relatively fit man and tried to fight back, but his strength paled in comparison to Goliath's brute power. It was like a house cat trying to fight a grizzly bear. Two brain-blasting blows to Ted's jaw knocked him three-quarters of the way back into unconsciousness. The woman in the cage knew Goliath had pulled his punches. If he had struck Ted full force, he would have cracked the man's skull like an eggshell. She had seen it happen more than once.

Goliath stretched the semiconscious Ted face down on the table, still slick with his wife's blood, and held him there as Doc approached with a scalpel in hand. Patch and Honcho each grabbed hold of one of Ted's legs.

"Can't have you running away on us," Honcho grunted as Doc went to work.

The scalpel blade cut into the back of Ted's left heel and sliced deep until it severed the thick Achilles tendon, the fibers popping apart like a slashed rubber band. He repeated the grisly, crippling process on the right heel. Ted screamed as the sharp, agonizing pain jolted him awake. Doc smiled as blood streamed from the opened flesh and Ted's screams reverberated through the cabin like the cries of the damned, which is exactly what they were.

Up in the corner, the spider sank its fangs into the moth, driving deadly needles into the soft body to feed, oblivious to the savagery below.

———

The bonfire burned high and bright, flames leaping off the logs and casting flickering shadows into the intertwined canopy of pine boughs overhead. Mike and Carson sat in Adirondack chairs on the side of the fire that didn't blow smoke in their faces. Neither had said much since arriving at the hunting cabin, but Mike was just happy that his son wasn't tearing into him. He could deal with the silent treatment more easily than the cutting words and bitter accusations.

Mike squashed a melting marshmallow between two graham crackers and took a bite. He realized he had forgotten the chocolate, but decided he didn't really care. "Oh, man, that's good," he said appreciatively. "If I get to Heaven and find out they don't serve s'mores, I'm asking to go somewhere else."

"You seem pretty sure you've got a shot at Heaven for someone who did what you did," Carson said, breaking off a piece of Hershey's bar. He had already eaten at least half a dozen S'mores and showed no signs of slowing down. Clearly, the four hot dogs he had crammed down his gullet at dinner hadn't filled him up.

Mike gazed solemnly at his son. "If I go to Hell for letting your mom die, I deserve it, no argument about that."

"Well, at least we agree on something," Carson replied.

Mike shook his head. How many times would this cycle continue? They'd only been together for half a day, and it was already getting old. He looked for forgiveness, but Carson responded with bitter, cutting anger, and nothing ever changed. As the fire crackled and popped, Mike wished things could be different, but doubted they ever would be. Carson seemed rigid in his loathing, determined to resent his father until the end of his days.

"You ever going to forgive me?" Mike asked. The S'more seemed to abruptly lose its flavor, and he tossed it in the fire. The melting marshmallow sizzled in the flames. "Or is this rough patch gonna last forever?"

Carson's voice was tight and flat as he replied, "You basically killed my mother. Kind of hard to forgive and forget that skeleton rattling around in your closet."

Mike winced. The word *skeleton* made him think of Lisa, six feet underground in a casket, no doubt nothing but bones by now. He stared into the fire, shadows dancing over his face, as a single tear slid down his cheek. He turned his head to hide his shame.

The silence stretched, heavy and unrelenting. Carson stared into the flames as if searching for some kind of answer. "You think I don't want to let this go?" he finally said. "You think I don't wish I could wake up tomorrow and just...just be done with it? Go back to the way it was, act like everything's normal, like you didn't completely and utterly fail her?"

Mike didn't speak. He didn't trust himself *to* speak. He knew there was nothing he could say that would make it better. Silence seemed like the best option at the moment.

Carson barked out a bitter laugh. "I used to think it would feel good, holding onto all this rage, all this pain, all this anger. God knows you deserved it. Hell, you *still* deserve it. But the truth is, it hasn't made anything better. I can hate you 'til the day I die, and who knows, maybe I will. But it won't bring Mom back."

Mike swallowed hard, his throat tight. "No, it won't."

Carson leaned back in his chair and exhaled a long sigh. "Listen, Dad, I'll try to let go of the past, but it won't be easy for me. That being said, deep down, I know you didn't kill Mom. *He* killed her. The man in the ski mask. The man with the dragon on his gun. He's the one who pulled the trigger, not you."

His voice wasn't exactly warm and compassionate, but it was the least-cold Mike had heard it in a long, long time.

"I was scared, more than you can ever imagine, and so I let her die," Mike said quietly. "I was a coward, Carson. There's no other way to put it. I know it, and you know it. And I also know that it'll take a miracle for you to ever truly forgive me, but a miracle is what I'm asking for."

Carson said nothing. He just stared at the flames, his jaw tensing slightly like he was grinding his teeth. After a moment, he reached over and put a hand on his father's shoulder for just the briefest of moments.

Then, standing up, he muttered, "A miracle is what it's gonna take for us to get out of bed at the crack of dawn to hunt if we don't get some shuteye. Let's hit the sack. The varmints get up early, and so do we."

Mike awoke a few minutes before the alarm on his phone was set to blare at 5:00 a.m. He allowed his eyes to adjust to the lack of light as he listened to Carson snoring away in his sleeping bag, probably dreaming about bagging his limit of squirrels today—red squirrels only, since gray squirrels weren't in season yet—or maybe dropping a coyote.

He swung his legs over the side of his bunk and peered at the clock. As he did so, he thought he glimpsed sudden, furtive movement outside the small octagonal window above the dresser. He padded over in his bare feet to peer outside. The glass was fogged over, and he reached up to wipe it off. But the moisture wasn't on the inside of the pane, it was on the outside.

Like someone or something had been breathing on it.

Mike peered outside, but it was too dark to see much. He could barely make out the nearest trees, and they were less than fifteen yards away. He stared at the slowly dissipating patch of fog on the glass again.

A bear? Or maybe a Sasquatch?

He grinned at the thought. He had heard reports of Sasquatch sightings to the southeast, down in the Ticonderoga and Dresden areas, but never this far north. He wasn't sure he believed in the existence of such creatures, but he did wonder from time to time what he would do if he encountered one in the woods—crap his pants, was the most likely answer.

The buzz of the alarm interrupted his thoughts. He stopped thinking about the fogged-up window and started thinking about popping some squirrels and maybe trying his spaghetti with squirrel-meat sauce for supper tonight. He silenced the alarm and heard Carson squirming in his bunk with lots of moans and groans as he went through the waking-up process.

"Rise an' shine," Mike said in an exaggerated drawl. "Daylight's a-wastin'."

"There's no daylight yet," Carson grumbled sleepily.

"Early bird gets the worm," Mike replied. "Early hunter gets the game."

As Carson climbed out of his bunk, he muttered, "Yeah, but don't forget, the early worm gets eaten."

Mike chuckled and began pulling on his hunting clothes.

Mike whipped up a big batch of scrambled eggs, venison sausage, and home fries, cooked in enough butter to send cholesterol levels skyrocketing and washed down with black coffee strong enough to grow hair on a concrete block. The combination of greasy food and bitter brew ensured they both made pre-hunt trips to the outhouse, Carson warning that if he got bit on the ass by a spider, he was leaving.

Bellies full and guts purged, they checked their walkie-talkies to ensure their frequencies were synchronized—no cell phone service in this part of the woods—and then walked up the trail with Mike lecturing about various safety aspects of hunting. His primary point was that you needed to be positive you were shooting at a game animal and not another hunter hunkered in the brush. "If you're not sure, then don't pull the trigger," he said.

Carson rolled his eyes. "Yeah, Dad, I got it."

About a hundred and fifty yards past the cabin, the path split in two directions. Carson continued on the main path that would take him across a brook and parallel to a gully until he reached a series of beaver dams. Mike veered left after saying goodbye to his son, threading through some beech saplings at the base of a large hill—or small mountain, he couldn't tell which it was—until he found himself standing at the edge of a small, stagnant pond populated with dead trees and coated with green gunk. He circled the body of water and eventually settled in a thicket of oak trees overlooking an overgrown clear-cut that had been logged off years ago and allowed to brush over.

It was an ideal area for squirrels and rabbits. Mike wasn't a diehard hunter, but he knew enough to judge an area and ascertain whether or not it potentially held game. Rabbits technically weren't in season for another month or so, but he didn't rule out popping one if it showed up. Wild hare roasted over a campfire would taste great for dinner tonight, and he highly doubted any game wardens bothered patrolling this far back in the Scar Lake region.

The colors of dawn streaked the sky as he settled on a stump that boasted a thick layer of moss on top, forming a natural cushion. It was softer than some armchairs he had sat in. He settled in, laid his rifle across his knees, and waited for the red squirrels—or out-of-season rabbits—to show up for their morning browse. While he had opted for a shotgun for Carson, he himself preferred to plink away with a tube-fed .22 semi-automatic rifle. More of a challenge. And when you did bag something, you didn't have to waste time picking shotgun pellets out of the meat.

Comfortable and satisfied with his location, Mike simply relaxed and let the morning unfold around him. Off to his left, a button-head buck stepped out from behind a vine-crusted boulder, gave him a look, and bolted away without a backward glance. Somewhere in the distance, crows cawed, and a wild turkey gobbled, then much closer, chickadees started flitting through the branches and singing their morning song. The black flies showed up, too, buzzing near his head and face. He regretted leaving the bug spray back at camp.

Waving away the annoying insects, he never sensed the danger looming behind him until a large shadow suddenly enveloped him. A twig snapped, and Mike felt a surge of fear as he turned on the stump to face the threat.

A hatchet swung down at his head, sharp steel whistling through the air.

Mike's reaction was instant and instinctive.

He raised his hand to block the blow.

The blade struck him between the middle and ring fingers and split his palm open all the way down to the wrist. Blood spurted onto the ground as flesh and bone were severed.

Shocked, Mike didn't feel any pain. Didn't scream. He just stared at his wounded hand, cut in two like a piece of firewood. The .22 rifle slipped from his lap and fell in the dirt.

A huge, hulking man with arms like tree trunks raised the hatchet again. Mike heard someone yell, "Don't kill him, asshole!"

Whoever was yelling, the giant wasn't listening.

With an animalistic grunt, the brute planted the hatchet blade in the top of Mike's head in a perfectly delivered death stroke.

Mike's final thought as the hatchet crunched through his skull was, *Forgive me, Carson.*

Goliath watched the gore geyser from the dead man's chopped-open head. Brain matter always reminded him of cottage cheese, for some reason. As he yanked the hatchet free, the corpse fell off the stump and onto the blood-splattered ground, feet twitching in a spastic death dance.

Patch trotted over and smacked him on the shoulder. "You stupid dickhead, what'd you do that for? You planning on carrying the body all the way back to the cabin?"

Goliath shrugged and grunted. "Felt like killing something."

"Yeah, well, you killed the shit outta this guy."

"Quit your whining." Goliath wiped the bloody

hatchet on Mike's shirt and slid it through his belt. "I'll carry him back."

Patch shook his head. "Forget it. Let's just go get the kid. Between him and those two hikers, there's plenty of meat and organs for the next shipment. No point in working up a sweat dragging this dead loser through the woods."

"Honcho's gonna be pissed."

"Ask me if I give a rat's ass."

Goliath gestured at the corpse. "So, we just leave him here?"

Patch nodded as he leaned over and grabbed the fallen .22 rifle. As he straightened up, he said, "The bears and coyotes will take care of him. Few days from now, he'll be nothing but bones and gristle."

Carson had worked up a sweat and was panting a bit from exertion by the time he reached his hunting spot. The trail for the last couple hundred yards had gradually steepened and let him know that he wasn't in prime physical condition. *Should've spent more time working out on the weight pile in juvie,* he thought, *and less time playing poker for commissary items.*

He found a stump on a hardwood ridge that was loaded with both red and white oak trees. Most of the acorns remained on the branches, but some had fallen to the forest floor. Piles of pebbled deer scat littered the leaves, proving this was a popular place for the whitetail bucks, does, and fawns to feed. Too bad they weren't in season. He could go for some venison right about now.

He settled down, enjoying the stillness of the woods at dawn, and let the thoughts come, just like he had known they would. When he was alone like this, all he could think about was his dead mother, his cowardly father, and the years he had spent locked up.

He knew his dad was trying to make things right. Maybe trying too hard, truth be told. The new shotgun was a nice enough gesture, despite Carson's dismissive reaction to it, but the only thing that had a chance of healing the wounds between them was time. Still, at least he was trying. Carson had not been lying at the campfire last night. He really didn't want to feel this way forever. He had lost his mother and was pretty much estranged from his father, and that was no way to live.

He suddenly slapped the side of his neck. When he pulled his hand back, a small splat of blood stained his palm. He also spotted some tiny, twisted legs and crushed wings mixed into the mess. "Stupid mosquitoes," he muttered. Still, he would rather deal with mosquitoes than deer flies. Those things frigging hurt when they bit you.

He was wiping off his hand on his pants when he heard something crashing through the trees toward him. The noise was loud, all crackling leaves and snapping twigs and breaking branches. Whatever it was, it was coming his way fast. He grabbed the shotgun, clicked off the safety, and pointed the barrel in the direction of the crashing sounds. His heart hammered, spiked on adrenaline, as he waited for whatever was charging toward him to appear. *Please, God, don't let it be a bear. How about a moose? I could deal with a moose. But if it* is *a bear, help me make a perfect kill shot, right between the eyes. I don't want to die out here.*

He didn't even think about the fact that the small game shells in the shotgun wouldn't do much to stop a charging bear.

The noise grew louder and louder...and then completely stopped.

Carson remained still, but his eyes flicked back and forth in their sockets, peering into the woods. He waited for what seemed like several minutes, but was probably no more than thirty seconds. Finally, when nothing appeared, he lifted the shotgun to his shoulder and peered through the scope. With the magnification dialed all the way up to 9X, whatever he viewed through the scope was brought into much closer focus, but it also significantly narrowed his field of vision.

Keeping his eyes glued to the scope, he swung the shotgun slowly to the left, scanning the trees, the rocks, the brush.

Nothing.

I know I heard something.

He swung the shotgun back to the right, and a woman's bloody head suddenly filled his crosshairs. One second, she wasn't there, the next she popped into frame like some kind of gruesome jack-in-the-box. Carson nearly jumped out of his skin.

"Holy shit!" he yelped.

Her forehead, cheeks, and arms were covered with slashes that looked like somebody had gone at her with a knife. Some were scabbed over, but others appeared fresh. Blood streaked her face into a red mask, and more blood stained her torn and shredded shirt. Carson lowered the gun as the woman screamed, "Help me! Please help me!"

Carson rose from the stump and took a step backward, not quite sure what to make of the injured woman in front of him. "Who are you?" he said, though he could reasonably guess that she was the Sonya Sawyer signed into the logbook at the trailhead. "What happened?" There seemed to be no immediate threat, so he slung the shotgun over his shoulder.

The woman stared at him for a moment. She seemed

dazed, maybe from blood loss. Then she blinked and rushed toward him.

"Hey, lady, are you okay?" he asked, taking another automatic step back, retreating from the woman's panicked charge.

He didn't move fast enough. Sonya closed the gap, and her hand shot out to grab his arm, fingers digging desperately into the sleeve of his shirt. Carson tried to pull away, but her grip was strong. The woman was clearly half-crazed out of her mind. "Please!" she said frantically. "Come with me! They're going to kill him! Please, you have to help!"

Kill? Did she just say kill? Carson tried to take another step back, but Sonya's other hand reached out and grabbed his arm, holding him in place. "Relax, lady," Carson said. "You need to take a breath, calm down, and then tell me what the hell is going on. Who's gonna kill you? Go with you where?"

The woman abruptly let go of him. "This way!" she said, hurrying back the way she had just came from. Not really a path, but more like a game trail.

"Hold on." Carson grabbed his walkie-talkie, keyed the mic, and said, "Dad, you there?"

He heard a squelch of static and then Sonya darted back and slapped the radio out of his hand. He glared at her as the unit broke into pieces on the rocks at his feet. Pieces of shattered casing and busted circuitry bounced against his boots.

"There's no time for that!" The woman practically screamed the words.

"What the hell is wrong with you?" Carson snapped.

"There's no time! We have to hurry! They're going to kill him!"

"Maybe I should go get my father first."

"There's no time!"

Sonya was starting to sound like a broken record. "All right, I got it, there's no time," Carson said. "Let's go." He took the shotgun off his shoulder and made sure there was a shell in the chamber as he followed the bloody woman deeper into the woods.

TWELVE

BRANCHES REACHED out and clutched at Carson like skeletal hands, and thorny brush clawed at his clothes as he followed Sonya's hurtling flight down the path. Blood dripped from her cuts every few yards and stained the earth beneath their running feet. Normally, it would have been hard not to stare at her wounds, but he was too busy trying not to stumble and break an ankle. The open woods had given way to far more rugged terrain, but Sonya showed no sign of slowing down.

Carson was really starting to huff, the lactic burn searing his muscles, and was just about to ask, "How much farther?" when they threaded their way between two huge boulders and burst out of the brush into a small hollow where a ramshackle cabin stood. The place looked old, as if it had been built by mountain hermits back in the 1800s.

His foot kicked against something half-buried in the dirt. He looked down and saw a skull grinning up at him, patches of white bone showing through the wormy earth.

Fear uncoiled in his guts and began a slow-crawl through his system. "What is this place?" he asked. He had been in some tough spots behind the razor wire, but some primal instinct warned him that he had never been as screwed as he was right now.

"I'm sorry, so sorry. They said they would let us go if I brought you here. I'm sorry, so, so sorry." Sonya was babbling, and Carson knew that was never a good sign. "I'm so, so sorry, but I really didn't have a choice."

"What are you talking about?" Carson demanded. "*Who* are you talking about?"

Sonya pointed over his shoulder. "Him!"

Carson turned just in time to catch a haymaker flush on the jaw. The blow spun him around so fast that the shotgun went sailing away to land in the dirt. A second later, Carson's unconscious body joined it.

When he regained consciousness, Carson found himself still sprawled in the dirt, but now his hands and feet were bound by thick ropes. They were tied tight enough to cut off his circulation. Somebody clearly knew their way around knots.

His head pounded with pain from the punch that had knocked him out. He felt a little nauseous and wondered if he had a concussion. Wouldn't have surprised him, as that blow had been vicious. He coughed to clear his dry throat and then rolled onto his side and up onto his knees. His vision swam, and he shook his head to clear it.

When the blurriness receded, he saw Sonya standing nearby. There were four men—the one who knocked him out, a hulking brute, a bald guy with an eyepatch, and one smaller man—gathered around her. Two of the men, the little guy and Eyepatch, held up a fifth man. It took Carson a few moments to realize why the fifth man couldn't stand on his own—the back of his ankles had been hacked open, the wound raw and ugly.

During their urgent flight through the woods, Carson had pieced together from Sonya's babblings that she had been hiking with her husband, Ted, so he assumed that was who the crippled man was. He looked like he was in rough shape, like he already had one tendon-clipped foot in the grave and all it would take was a soft puff from the Reaper to put him in the rest of the way.

"I did what you asked." Sonya's plaintive voice pleaded with the tall guy who seemed to be the leader, a sawed-off shotgun dangling from a shoulder sling. "I brought him here, just like you wanted. So please, let us go, like you promised."

The leader stared at her with a cruel smile that made his face ugly. Not that it was much to look at to begin with. "You want me to let him go?"

Sonya nodded. "Yes. Please."

Carson could tell plain as day what was coming next. Had she not been hanging onto her last strand of desperate hope, Sonya no doubt would have seen it too. But instead, she never saw it coming.

The leader looked over at the two men holding Ted and gave them a nod. They let go of the helpless man, who immediately dropped to his knees, head lolling weakly forward until his chin touched his chest. In one violent blur of motion, the smaller guy whipped out a scalpel, jerked Ted's head back, and sliced his throat wide open with a quick, clean, surgical cut. Clearly not the killer's first rodeo. Carson saw the flesh gape and the blood gush.

"NOOOOO!" Sonya screamed. The horrible cry ricocheted off the boulders surrounding the hollow and echoed back like a torturous taunt.

Ted clutched at his slashed throat for a moment, his

fingers funneling the spraying blood into jets, and then toppled onto his face. He exhaled his final breath in a wet gurgle as the ground beneath him turned to crimson mud.

Sonya threw herself at the leader in a grief-stricken rage, pounding her fists against his chest as she screamed, "You bastard! You promised!" But that outburst sapped her last reserves of strength, and she slid to the ground, kneeling in front of her captor, arms now hanging limply at her side. "You promised," she whimpered. "You promised you would let us go." She sounded betrayed, as if she had actually believed the pack of killers would keep their word.

The leader sneered down at the woman on her knees before him, then grabbed his sawed-off shotgun and rammed it into her face. "I should shove this down your throat and pull the trigger," he growled. "Watch your pretty little head come apart."

Sonya looked up at him with terrified eyes as he pressed the muzzle against her upper lip. She whimpered at the touch of cold steel. The leader's finger toyed with the trigger. Carson winced, fully expecting a shotgun blast to detonate Sonya's skull at any second.

She was clearly broken. She just closed her eyes and waited for the end, waited for it to be over, no fight left in her at all. When her tormentor finally pulled the shotgun away and canted it over his shoulder, she fell forward, sobbing. Then she lifted her miserable face and looked up at the man wearily as if to say, *What next?*

Carson half-expected the leader to say, "Just kidding," and whip the shotgun back into play and execute Sonya right then and there. But instead, he pointed toward the woods beyond the boulders and growled, "Go on, get outta here."

Sonya looked shocked. "You're...you're not going to kill me?"

"Go," the man snapped. "Now. Before I change my mind."

She slowly climbed to her feet, flinching at every movement, clearly expecting a shotgun blast to end her life at any moment. She looked toward the woods and took a hesitant step forward.

The leader rammed the shotgun into her chest and gave her a rough shove. "Go!" he roared. "Won't tell you again."

Sonya turned and sprinted blindly into the woods. Carson watched her disappear from sight and hoped he never saw her again.

Sonya didn't know which direction to run, but right now that didn't matter. All that mattered was that against all odds, she was free. Getting away from her captors—and Ted's killers—was not her primary goal, it was her *only* goal. The thick brush blocked her vision, and thorns tore at her skin, but she kept forcing her way forward.

Her freedom lasted for several hundred yards before coming to an abrupt halt. She never saw the bear trap camouflaged beneath a screen of leaves and branches. Running in blind, panicked flight, she put her foot squarely down on the plate. The massive steel jaws snapped shut just below her knee, the metal teeth easily shearing through flesh and muscle and biting all the way to the bone. She jerked to a stop and screamed in pain.

She kept on screaming until the giant, hulking beast of a man emerged from the trees with a hatchet in his hand, whistling tunelessly. And then the scream died—along with Sonya—as the hatchet went up and then came down and cleaved her skull nearly in half.

Goliath removed the body from the bear trap by reaching down and pushing the metal jaws the rest of the way through the tibia, severing the leg. He then grabbed the remaining leg and began dragging the corpse back to the cabin. Doc would harvest the organs, and then they would let Ted and Sonya's bodies hang like a fresh-killed deer for a few days to age the meat. The wealthy buyer up in Canada preferred it that way. Claimed it added *subtle textual nuances* to the taste of the flesh.

THIRTEEN

FOUR DAYS LATER...

STONE KNEW a hard man when he saw one.

Not the small-town tough-guy kind of hard, the local bully who won a few amateur boxing bouts and fancied himself a badass, the high school football player that never grew up and spent the rest of his stunted life shoving people around or breaking legs for mobsters. No, that kind of bargain-basement hardness barely registered with Stone.

The ones that set off his radar were the men who lived by the gun, the lethal warrior types who wore a dangerous, predatory aura like a cloak. The kind of man who had been to hell and back, who had ridden hard through the flames, spit in the devil's eye, and lived to tell about it. The kind of man who walked around with haunted eyes that were both sorrowful and primal.

Like the man Stone saw walking out of the Nailed Coffin bar on Friday afternoon.

Stone had just finished up a call about a disorderly man at the hospital, throwing a water bottle at a volunteer, and was on his way back to the station to type up the report, grumpy about the thought of more paperwork. As he stopped at the intersection by the Nailed Coffin and drummed his fingers on the steering wheel of his '78 Chevy Blazer while he waited for the light to turn green, he saw the man step out of the bar. He looked to be in his late forties, tall and rangy, with hair that was more gray than black, buzzed short, a thick mustache that curled down over the corners of his mouth, and plenty of facial stubble. Their eyes locked, and you could practically feel the crackle between them as each man recognized the other for what they were.

A soldier, warrior, operator, hunter, fighter, whatever you wanted to call it.

The passenger side window was down to let in some air to combat the late summer heat. Stone leaned over and called out, "Can I give you a lift?"

"Got my own ride," the man said. No menace in his voice, but plenty of caution.

"Then can I buy you a beer?"

The man jerked a thumb over his shoulder at the bar behind him. "Just had one."

"Have another."

"One's my limit these days."

"I get that," Stone said. "Listen, I'm not looking to give you trouble. Just looking for a conversation."

"I'm not much of a talker."

The light turned green. The car behind Stone honked to let him know. Stone kept his foot on the brake and looked at the hard man. "Will you stop giving me grief and just get in the truck?"

The guy shook his head ruefully, stepped off the curb, and climbed into the Chevy as the traffic light turned yellow. Stone gunned through the intersection, and in his rearview mirror, saw the person driving the car behind him flip him off. *Yeah, I had that one coming.*

"Got a name?" Stone asked the man now riding shotgun.

"I can give you one, but you and I both know it'll be faker than a porn star's orgasm."

"Gotta call you something."

"Call me Wade."

"Last name?"

"Garrett."

Stone shot him a sideways glance. "Like the cooler from *Road House*?"

"You know your '80s action movies."

"Now that you mention it, you do kind of resemble Sam Elliot."

"I'll take that as a compliment."

"You should," Stone said. "Now, since you won't let me buy you a beer, can I buy you something else while we talk?"

"Got any ice cream in this backwater town?"

"Ice cream?"

"Yeah," Garrett replied. "It's hot as hell, and I could go for a hot fudge sundae."

Stone chuckled. "I've met my fair share of badass trigger pullers in my time, but never once did any of them ask for ice cream."

"You judging me?"

Stone shook his head. "Not really my style. One hot fudge sundae, coming right up."

"Since you're buying," Garett said, "make sure they give me extra peanuts."

Fifteen minutes later, they were sitting on the spacious covered deck that overlooked a large pond at Nature's Frost, the most popular seasonal ice cream stand in the Whisper Falls area, if not all of Garrison County. They sat in the corner, as far away from the other occupied tables, giving them the privacy Stone required.

He watched in amusement as Garrett tore into his hot fudge sundae—with extra peanuts—with the relish of a little kid. "This is really good," the man said. "I've had hot fudge sundaes all over the country, and this is right up there with the best of them."

"You got a hot fudge sundae fetish or something?" Stone asked.

Garrett shrugged. "We all need hobbies, right? A way to unwind?" He shot Stone a knowing look. "Especially in our line of work."

"Not sure what you're insinuating. I'm just a small-town preacher who moonlights as the sheriff."

"Yeah, right." Garrett shoveled another spoonful of fudge-dripping vanilla ice cream into his mouth. After swallowing that down the hatch, he said, "And I'm the damn tooth fairy." He finished the sundae, pushed the empty plastic bowl to the side, folded his arms on the table in front of him, and said, "Let's cut the bullshit, shall we? I know what you are, and you know what I am, so go ahead and ask your questions and let's get this sitrep over with."

Stone nodded. He liked Garrett's style. "How long you been in the game?"

"Joined the Army at nineteen. Did twenty years. Been a private contractor ever since."

"A merc."

Garrett shrugged. "Call it what you will."

"You didn't get that look in your eye by being a

regular Army soldier for twenty years," Stone said. "Rangers or Delta?"

"Ranger. You?"

"Bounced around the military branches." It wasn't exactly the truth, but it was as close as Stone cared to get.

Garrett saw right through it. "You were a black ops boy."

"It's a free country, so you can think what you want and let your imagination run wild."

"How does somebody like you end up in a place like this?" Garrett asked.

"Long story. You want to tell me what brings *you* to a place like this?"

"You asking as the sheriff, or as a fellow soldier?"

"The latter, mostly. Not often I see a guy like you in Whisper Falls."

"I tell you what I'm doing here, you gonna fuck up my op?"

"Depends. You here to kill somebody?"

Garrett shook his head. "I'm not that kind of merc. I don't do assassinations."

"Planning on hurting anybody?"

Garrett shrugged. "Possible, if that's what it takes to achieve the objective, but it's not the primary purpose."

"Then I doubt I'll have any reason to get in your way," Stone said.

"Good enough for me." Garrett leaned back in his chair. "I'm here to find a pair of missing persons."

"Names?"

"Michael and Carson Donner."

"They're not back from Scar Lake yet?"

"Not according to Mike's brother-in-law."

One of the pieces clicked into place for Stone. "You were hired by Mason Xavier."

"Know him?"

"Yeah, I know him," Stone replied. "He's not one of the good guys, Garrett."

Another shrug from Garrett. "Men like me can't always afford to be picky about where our next paycheck comes from. This Mason guy's not asking me to do anything illegal, just track down his brother-in-law and nephew."

"It's still dirty money."

"I hear you," Garrett said. "You hearing *me*?"

"I'm not trying to stop a man from making a living," said Stone. "And Xavier's right to be worried—Scar Lake is some rough country, and Mike and Carson should have been back days ago."

"Right." Garrett nodded. "So, if we're done here, I'd like to head up there and start looking for them."

"Want backup? Someone to watch your six?"

"Appreciate the offer, but I work better alone."

"You sure?"

"Give me your card. If I find myself up shit creek looking for a paddle, I'll give you a holler." After Stone slid him a business card, the mercenary pushed back his chair and stood up. "Thanks for the sundae." He grinned. "Hopefully it wasn't my last meal."

FOURTEEN

FIVE HOURS LATER, Wade Garrett—not his real name, obviously, but the one he always gave people when he didn't want them to know his true identity—found himself moving at a deliberate, measured pace through the woods to the southwest of the Burke cabin. He had extensive tracking experience, and since the Donner father-son duo weren't skilled woodsmen, their trail had been relatively easy to pick up. Scuffs in the dirt, partial footprints in the mud, broken branches, kicked over rocks, matted vegetation…it all coalesced together to form a picture that a knowledgeable tracker could use to ascertain the route taken.

When he reached the point where the two trails diverged, he had a decision to make. While he was a damn good tracker, he wasn't so good that he could tell which sign had been left by Mike and which had been left by Carson. Mason Xavier had made it bluntly clear that he cared far more about getting his nephew back than his brother-in-law. In fact, his exact words had been, *"If you find my brother-in-law, just put a bullet in his worthless head and leave him to rot, and I'll add an extra fifty percent to your fee."*

Of course, Garrett had declined. He had not been lying to Sheriff Stone when he said he wasn't an assassin. Not that he was a pacifist or anything like that. He would kill when necessary, either in self-defense or to rescue an innocent, but he didn't take money for the sole purpose of executing people.

With no way of knowing which path Carson took, Garrett opted to go left. He didn't even have a gut instinct, so he just made a random choice. Didn't even bother flipping a coin.

He followed the sign left behind by whoever had come this way, slowly approaching each bend in the trail, scanning ahead for threats. He had strapped a small knapsack to his back that held various survival gear, including waterproof matches and a basic first aid kit. It also contained three spare magazines, fully loaded with 9mm cartridges, for the SIG Sauer M17 pistol strapped to his side in a nylon tactical holster. It was counterbalanced on his left side by an SRK fixed-blade knife in a leather sheath.

He briefly wondered if he should have brought more firepower. Xavier had warned him about the teenage girl getting killed by the black bear last year. With their penchant for ricocheting off hard surfaces, a 9mm bullet might just deflect off a bear's thick skull instead of penetrating through to the brain, which would leave the bear royally pissed and Garrett saying, *Oh, shit!* God knew he didn't want to get into a knife fight with an angry bruin.

But he also knew that bears, especially black bears, rarely attacked humans, and he hadn't felt like lugging the extra weight of a rifle around this godforsaken backcountry.

He followed the trail another two hundred yards and

came to an oak grove near a clear-cut. He thought he spotted something up ahead, lying near a moss-covered stump, but before he could check it out, the hairs on the back of his neck prickled. He spun to check behind him, hand falling to the butt of his SIG as his sixth sense put him on high alert. Not spooked—too many years in bad situations to get spooked easily—but he definitely felt like something was wrong.

His eyes moved rapidly in their sockets, scanning the terrain. He didn't see anybody, but he did hear some rustling in the thick tree canopy above him. He glanced up to see a gray squirrel plucking acorns from the high branches. He knew the little tree-hopping rodents found the tasty attraction of acorns impossible to resist, and evening was prime feeding time. He watched the squirrel hop from branch to branch, making the leaves shake.

"I ought to blow your furry little ass into stew meat," he muttered. He seriously considered popping the squirrel and roasting it over a fire tonight for dinner. But if Mike and Carson Donner had been taken by hostile forces, he didn't want to alert those forces to his presence by firing a shot. He would just stick with the provisions he had packed in.

He moved forward to check out whatever was lying by the stump—now that he was closer, it looked like a decomposing body, and he wondered if maybe his rescue mission was going to turn into a corpse retrieval—and carefully avoided stepping on twigs that would snap under his boots.

Then he heard a twig snap behind him.

He turned, moving fast, reaching for his sidearm.

But the man with the sawed-off shotgun already had his finger on the trigger.

Garrett managed to get the SIG out of the holster just as the shotgun's thunderous roar cannoned through the woods. The blast took him high on the right side of his chest, where the arm and shoulder connected. He felt the buckshot tearing flesh and shattering bone. With the socket destroyed, the pistol tumbled from his fingers and fell to the ground.

The impact spun him around almost one hundred and eighty degrees, just in time to see another man step out from behind a tree. This one sported an eyepatch and held a .357 Magnum in his hand. The revolver was raised and pointed right at Garrett.

They pincered me, he thought through the pain. *Bullets from both sides.*

The Magnum bucked in the one-eyed man's fist. Garrett tried not to cry out in pain, but couldn't help it as a bullet blew apart his knee. The left leg buckled, dropping him to the ground, that was now spattered with his blood.

The man with the eyepatch casually strolled toward him. Garrett craned his neck and saw the shotgun-wielder closing in from behind him. *I might be down, but I'm not out of the fight yet, you miserable shit-suckers.* He used his left hand to reach for his fallen pistol. Like any halfway decent operator, he could shoot a gun with either hand. All part of the training.

The shotgun roared again, and Garrett saw—and felt—his left hand vaporized like some kind of grisly magic trick. There one second, gone the next. Nothing remained below the wrist but ragged strips of flesh and shredded bone.

He didn't cry out this time. The pain barely even registered. *Shock,* he realized. *I'm going into shock, goddamn it.*

The man with the shotgun came over and nonchalantly booted the SIG out of arm's reach. It bounced off a tree trunk several yards away. Not that it mattered much anymore. He let the sawed-off blaster dangle down by his side as he studied Garrett and asked, "Exactly who the fuck are you?"

Garrett suffered no delusions and understood the grim reality of his situation. He was a dead man and he damn well knew it. So, he answered the question. "Came for the man and the boy. Mike and Carson Donner."

"What, you some kind of badass tracker or something?"

"Tracker, yeah. Badass, maybe not so much. Not if I let a couple of amateurs like you get the drop on me."

"Amateurs?" The shotgunner chuckled. "We know this godforsaken backcountry better than you know your own pecker. We're like ghosts or fucking forest fairies—you won't see us unless we want you to. You could take a full-blooded Apache warrior from the 1800s and plop him down here and even he wouldn't be able to get the drop on us."

"They know I'm here," Garrett said, knowing he was wasting his time but taking a stab at not getting killed anyway. "You pissed off a very rich and powerful guy when you messed with his nephew. He's not going to stop sending people to find them. If I don't come back, he'll just send more. Plus, Sheriff Stone knows I came here looking for Mike and Carson. You kill me, these woods are gonna get real crowded, real quick."

"Stone?" the man with the eyepatch echoed. "That cowboy preacher-sheriff mashup over in Whisper Falls? I heard about him."

"That's the one," Garrett replied.

"Hell with him," the man with the shotgun snapped. "That's Garrison County. Stone doesn't have any jurisdiction here."

Garrett smiled grimly. "Not sure that matters much to a man like Stone."

"Guess we'll find out," the man said, teeth peeling back from his lips in a feral snarl. "Because you aren't gonna make it back."

Garrett saw the one-eyed man raise the .357 Magnum and thought, *Can't believe after all the shit I survived, I'm going out like this.*

Then the revolver roared and blew his head in half, and all his thoughts came to a sudden, shattering end.

The two men loomed over the crimson-coated corpse. Patch wiped sticky bits of tissue off his face and grunted, "That back-spray was a real bitch. Got stinking merc brains all over me."

"If that retarded merc had any brains, he wouldn't have come here bothering us," Honcho replied. "Stupid son of a bitch."

"Yeah, well, he ain't got no brains now, that's for sure. We hauling him back with us?"

Honcho shook his head. "The distributor won't be ready for another organ shipment for a few days."

"Right," Patch grunted. "Which is why we're still keeping that kid in the cage with the girl."

"That's part of the reason," Honcho replied. "But also, because the big bossman said he doesn't want the kid killed until he gets here."

"He going soft on us?"

"Soft is not a word I would use to describe the boss."

Patch gestured at Garrett's half-headless body on the ground. "What about the meat?"

"That rich prick in Canada doesn't need that much," Honcho replied. "We've already got those two hikers hanging in the shed, and we'll butcher the Donner kid after Doc is done harvesting his organs, so that should be plenty of meat for this shipment. You can leave this bitch-ass Rambo wannabe here with the boy's father." He gestured at Mike Donner's corpse over by the stump, not much more than bones after being scavenged the last several days. "The crows and coyotes can have him, for all I care."

FIFTEEN

STONE WAS EATING breakfast at the Birch Bark Diner when Mason Xavier walked in like he owned the place and headed straight for his table.

Stone had stopped by the diner hoping to run into Holly, but when he arrived, the other waitress informed him she had called in sick. The way she said it made it clear that the waitress believed Stone was the cause of the sickness. He had settled into his usual table, tucked into the corner so he could face the door with his back to the wall, and ordered a basic bacon-eggs-hashbrowns-toast breakfast, along with some coffee to wash down the disappointment he felt at Holly's absence.

And now, just to make a bad day even worse, he was going to have to deal with Mason Xavier. *You used to have Holly for a breakfast companion, and now you've got Xavier. Talk about a downgrade.*

The morning sun streamed through the large front windows of the diner and bathed the interior in a warm, golden light, a prelude to the shimmering heat that would show up in just a couple of hours. Outside, a light breeze caused dust to swirl across the parking lot.

Mason Xavier didn't seem to pay attention to any of those details as he pulled out a chair opposite Stone and sat down without waiting for an invitation. Probably because he knew Stone would never extend him one. His razor-cut black hair looked freshly groomed, but his face was haggard, and his usually impeccable suit looked like it could use an ironing. Maybe he had given the maid the day off.

"Sheriff, I need your help."

"Some folks might consider that rude," Stone said.

"Asking for help?"

"Sitting down at a man's table without being invited."

Xavier blinked. "Are you being serious right now?"

"I'm always serious at breakfast."

Xavier rolled his eyes, reached into his suit coat, pulled out a wad of cash, and tossed it on the table. "There, I'm buying. Does that make it all right for me to sit here and talk to you?"

Stone had a forkful of scrambled eggs in his right hand, but used his left to shove the money back toward Whisper Falls's notorious crime boss. "I don't want your money. Just tell me what you came here to say and then leave me alone."

"Like I said, I need your assistance."

"This about Wade Garrett?"

Xavier looked surprised. "You know about him?"

"Met him on his way through town. Let me guess—he didn't come back."

"He was supposed to check in last night and this morning, but I haven't heard from him. Radio silence, as you trigger pullers like to say."

"No cell service up in Scar Lake."

"He had a satphone."

"So not only are your brother-in-law and nephew missing, but so is the professional tracker you hired to find them." Stone washed down the eggs with a swig of coffee.

"That about sums it up, yes," Xavier replied.

What the hell is going on up in Scar Lake? Stone wondered. Aloud, he said, "Must sting like a bastard, coming to me for help."

"Obviously, you were not my first option," Xavier responded. "But I will do whatever is necessary to get Carson back."

"What about his father?"

Xavier shrugged. "You are a man who appreciates honesty, right? Well, if I'm being honest, I really could not care less about Michael Donner, the coward who let my sister die."

"I've heard the story and read the police report. He was faced with an impossible choice."

"No, not impossible," Xavier replied. "Difficult, yes… but not impossible. Are you going to sit there and tell me that if you and Holly were put in the same exact situation, that you wouldn't put a bullet in your head to save her?"

"I'm saying that not all men are built the same, and nobody can be sure what they'll do in a situation until the moment arrives."

Xavier made a dismissive motion with his hand. "Well, we can certainly agree on the first part of that statement. As for the second, well, that's a debate for another time."

"There won't be another time," Stone replied. "Eating breakfast with you is not going to be a regular thing."

"I don't care if you hate me," Xavier said. "Just as long as you help me. I may not *like* you very much, but I *respect* you as a man who gets things done. I need you to find Carson and Mike. Or, if you can't find them, at least find out what happened to them."

"Not my jurisdiction."

"Then don't do it as the sheriff, do it as the preacher. Lord knows you've got two sides, and honestly, I have no idea how you make that work. Besides, I'm willing to pay you, so you can just consider yourself a private contractor."

"I don't work for men like you," Stone said.

Xavier ignored the insult. "Name your price, Stone. Cash, land…hell, I'll even build you a brand-new church, if that's what it takes."

Stone kept his voice low and steady. "I'm not for sale, Mason."

Xavier held his gaze. "You're quite self-righteous for a man with a whole lot of blood on his hands."

"I'm the sheriff," Stone said, wondering why he was bothering to argue with this jerkoff. "I protect the community."

"By killing?"

"When necessary, yeah."

Xavier smiled thinly. "Oh, I think you and I both know that not all your kills have been *necessary*, but no need to go down that particular road today. However, it does lead me to another point." He leaned forward and dropped his voice to just above a whisper that wouldn't carry to anyone else in the diner. "Fact of the matter is, this isn't only about finding out what happened to Mike and Carson. You see, somebody messed with my family and whoever that somebody—or somebodies—is, I don't want them walking away."

Stone set down his fork and clenched his fists. Voice tight, he said, "You think I'm that kind of man? An assassin, a gunslinger, a hitter for hire? Someone who doesn't know the difference between justice and execution? That what you think, Mason?"

Xavier's thin, humorless smile remained intact.

"Don't for one moment think it's escaped my notice that not only are you not the typical preacher, you're also not the typical sheriff."

Stone heard Deputy Valentine's words echo in his head. *"You just seem to have a knack for finding more times and places to put men in coffins than any other lawman I've ever met."*

Stone didn't deny that his often-lethal brand of justice often existed outside the law. He also knew that it didn't really reconcile with scripture either, other than the fact that God called some men to be warriors. But he was learning to live with it, even when it troubled his spirit. More and more these days, he simply accepted who he was, *what* he was. A man whose sense of justice was often primal and unforgiving.

Xavier was still talking. "You're someone who understands that sometimes the law isn't enough, that the boundaries of civilization can sometimes lead to miscarriages of justice."

Stone just stared at him, eyes hard, jaw clenched.

"You're a man who doesn't believe evil deserves a second chance," Xavier added.

Stone turned his head and stared outside at the mountains rising in the distance, the majestic peaks crowned with warm sunlight that seeped down ridgelines to chase the shadows into the deepest gullies and ravines. Part of him hated that Mason Xavier was right, that Garrison County's biggest crime boss saw through Stone's civilized veneer at the hard, violent man beneath. Xavier might not know much about Stone's warrior past, about the dark years of spitting bullets and spilling blood in the world's nastiest shitholes, but he clearly sensed that Stone had a beast inside him that was only sleeping, not extinct.

But no matter what secrets Xavier had gleaned and

how much Stone wanted to prove him wrong, he couldn't just turn away when people's lives were at stake. He might despise having a man like Mason Xavier take his measure, but it really didn't matter. Somebody had to do the hard things to protect the innocent.

Stone turned away from the mountain view and fixed his eyes on Xavier again. "I'll go," he said. "But I'm not doing it for you. I'm doing it for Mike and Carson."

Xavier nodded. He showed no sign of gloating or victory in his posture, even though he had achieved what he had set out to do. "I meant what I said. I'll give you whatever you want."

All this I will give you if you bow down and worship me.

The words of the devil himself as he tempted Jesus in the wilderness.

Stone knew he was no Jesus, but he didn't give a damn about the devil's money either.

He stared at Xavier and growled, "Just shut your mouth, get up, and walk away before I change my mind."

With a quick nod, Xavier complied. As Stone watched the man exit the diner, he felt a heavy weight inside. But it was a familiar weight, the weight of a man with too much blood on his hands, the weight of a warrior who sometimes still wrestled with the balance between faith and fury.

He had come to this town looking for peace and redemption.

So far, he had found neither.

SIXTEEN

STONE FINISHED HIS BREAKFAST, paid his bill, tried calling Holly again, got no answer, said a quick prayer for a speedy resolution to his messed-up love life, and headed into town. He rolled down the window in the Chevy Blazer and hoped the fresh air and warm wind would chase away the heaviness he felt after his meeting with Xavier.

He hoped he had made it clear to the man that he wasn't working for him. He didn't need the crime boss getting any notion that he had somehow managed to get his hooks into Stone. If that's what he thought, he was sorely mistaken, because Stone bowed to no one but God.

But he couldn't just leave Mike and Carson Donner out there. Stone had been the one who suggested they go to Pastor Burke's cabin in Scar Lake, so he felt at least partially responsible for anything that might have happened to them.

And it seemed pretty clear that *something* had happened to them. Now it was just a matter of figuring out *what*.

He found a parking spot across from the post office

and strolled down the sidewalk toward his destination. He was greeted by townsfolk along the way, most of them remarking how hot it must be to wear a Stetson in this heat. He reminded them that he came from Texas, so he was used to it. Truth was, the Adirondacks didn't even come close to matching the eyeball-frying sizzle of a Texas summer. To say nothing of some of the desert hell-holes he had found himself in during his warrior days.

He waved through storefront windows as he passed, acknowledging the retailers and merchants that formed the backbone of Whisper Falls. This was truly a small town, dominated by locally owned businesses, with little sign of chain stores or corporations. The nearest Wal-Mart was almost an hour away, something that often shocked the tourists. Stone had no idea if this little town he now called home could resist the encroachment of modernism forever, but for now, it held fast to its quaintness with strength and dignity.

Stone passed the Jamaican food takeout place, the toy store, the bookshop, and a travel agency and arrived at his destination: Ruff Rick's Sporting Goods and Pet Supplies. For his search-and-rescue mission to Scar Lake, he planned on taking the Rossi Triple Black .30-30 lever-action rifle he had recently acquired, but needed to buy a couple boxes of ammo for it. He figured he might as well pick up a bag of dog food for Max at the same time.

Stone walked into Rick's and was greeted by the rich aroma of gunpowder and cleaning solvent. Rick had a pistol—looked like a Walther—disassembled on the counter and was busy wiping down the parts with an oily rag that looked like it might have been around during the Civil War. He looked up as Stone entered.

"Mornin', Sheriff."

"Morning, Rick. How's it going?"

"Be better if my willie was wet."

"Don't think I can help you with that."

Rick snorted. "C'mon, man, you're the sheriff. You know where all the best hookers hang out."

"Prostitution really isn't a big problem in this town."

"Far as I'm concerned, hookers are never a problem."

"Try hanging out at the Nailed Coffin. I'm sure an opportunity will present itself."

"See? I knew you'd know." Rick winked.

Stone smiled and shook his head. Rick was one of the town's genuine old-timers, just like Grizzle over at the Jack Lumber Bar & Grill. But where Griz dished out sage advice and hard-earned wisdom, Rick was more of the jester type, dropping lewd jokes with a dirty chuckle, a crooked grin, and mischievous eyes.

"So, you here on official business or personal?" Rick asked, pushing aside the broke-down pistol and flipping the dirty cleaning rag over his shoulder.

"Personal. Need a couple boxes of thirty-thirty."

"You want round nose, flat nose or hollow-points?"

"Hollow."

Rick arched a brow. "Lookin' for some serious take-down power, huh?"

"Heading up to Scar Lake to look for some missing people. Not sure what I'll run into up there, so figured I'd go with the hollow-points just in case."

"You going after the Donner boys?"

Stone nodded. "Yeah, how'd you know?"

"Mike came by last Sunday, I think it was, and bought a shotgun, told me he was headin' up there with his boy for a few days." Rick frowned. "Guess they never came back, huh?"

"Looks that way."

Rick shook his head. "That's some rough country up there. Not the first person to go missing in those parts.

Plus, that preacher's daughter got killed by the bear a ways back."

"Burke."

Rick looked puzzled. "Say what?"

"That's the preacher's name—Burke. Daughter's name was Jenny."

"Oh. Right. Rings a bell, now that you say it. Pastor over at a church in Bloomingdale, right?" Rick didn't wait for an answer. "Anyway, I'm guessing you know Scar Lake is some downright unfriendly terrain, full of thorns and thistles and all sorts of thick, nasty shit."

"That's why I'm sticking with the thirty-thirty," Stone replied.

Rick nodded. "Best brush gun ever created, far as I'm concerned."

"No argument from me."

"You go for the classic look, or are you one of those tactical junkies?"

Stone smiled. "Rossi Triple Black."

Rick snorted. "Should've known. You cops and soldier-types all get a hard-on whenever you see some black paint and picatinny rails on a rifle." He shook his head. "Tacticalizing a lever-action should be considered obscene, like pissing on the Bible or something."

"I don't think tacticalizing is a word," Stone said.

"It is now," Rick replied.

"Well," Stone said, "if we all liked the same thing, we'd all be married to the same woman, and that would just get awkward sometimes."

Rick snorted derisively. "Marriage is for fools and guys who can't pick up chicks at a bar."

"Cynical much?"

"Just a lifelong bachelor and proud of it." Rick turned to the shelves behind him, which looked ready to buckle under the weight of all the ammo boxes, and plucked a couple cartons of .30-30 cartridges from a stack. He set them on the counter.

"Thanks," Stone said, handing him some cash. "I'm gonna grab a bag of dog food on the way out, too."

Rick rang him out, gave him his change, and said, "Be careful up there in Scar Lake. They found our last sheriff's bones up in the mountains after he disappeared. Don't want them to find yours."

Stone kept his face unreadable. He knew all about the previous sheriff's bones, since he was the one who had killed the man. Or rather, kneecapped the bastard with a pair of bullets in the middle of a blizzard and left him for the coy-wolves to finish off. And the scumbag pedophiliac murderer had deserved every inch of agony he got.

To Rick, he said, "Not my first rodeo, but I'll be careful. Thanks for your concern."

Rick chuckled. "Maybe it's not concern. Maybe I just don't want to break in another sheriff."

SEVENTEEN

"MOM'S still wicked mad at you," Lizzy informed him.

The Blazer was packed and ready for the excursion to Scar Lake. Stone had considered bringing Max with him —the Shottie could use a little more exercise, having packed on a few extra pounds lately—but decided against it. He didn't know what he would encounter on this trip, and he didn't want to be worrying about the dog if things went sideways. *Think of it as a mission and eliminate all distractions.*

He'd called Lizzy to see if she would take care of Max and Rocky while he was gone. She had cheerfully said yes and then immediately let him know that Holly was still upset.

"I know," Stone said, grimacing. "But there's not much I can do about it if she doesn't want to talk to me."

"Go by the house and see her."

"I doubt she would answer the door."

"Then kick it in." Lizzy sighed. "Try harder, Luke. Waiting for her to come around obviously isn't working, in case you haven't noticed."

Never thought I'd be getting dating advice from a teenager, Stone thought.

He said, "I'll stop by before I leave, see if she'll talk to me."

"Make sure you're packing heat," Lizzy advised. "Way she feels right now, she might just shoot you through the door before you get a chance to say anything."

"That's nice."

"Where are you riding off to, anyway? Let me guess, saving the world again?"

Stone quickly explained the situation.

On the other end of the line, Lizzy sighed. "Why does it always have to be you doing the dangerous shit?"

"Dangerous shit is kind of my job, Liz."

"Not this time. Scar Lake isn't your jurisdiction."

"It's not a cop thing, it's a preacher thing. Mike Carson came to me with a problem, and I suggested he take his son up there. Now they're missing. I can't be a good shepherd if I'm not willing to protect my flock."

"You could just call the police up in Scar Lake and let them handle it."

"At the risk of sounding like an arrogant SOB, do you really think those cops are better at this sort of thing than I am?" Stone asked.

"No, but—"

"There are no *buts*, Lizzy. This is what I do, this is who I am."

Another sigh, long and heavy. The worry came through in her voice as she said, "I know it's what you do, who you are. The cowboy preacher, right? The holy gunslinger. I just wish somebody else could face down the bad guys once in a while. But it seems like it's always you."

"The world needs peacemakers, and it needs

warriors," Stone replied. "That's just the way God made things work. In case you haven't noticed, I'm not very good at making peace."

"Have you ever tried?" Lizzy asked with a teasing lilt in her voice.

"I know who I am, what I'm called to do. No point in fighting it."

"Fine, be that way." Yet another sigh, and Stone was starting to realize that nobody could sigh as dramatically as a teenage girl. "I'll take care of your mutt and your nag while you run around playing badass for Jesus."

"Don't be a little shit," Stone said, smiling. "It's not like that, and you know it."

"Whatever." He could practically hear her roll her eyes through the phone. "Just come back breathing, okay?"

"That's the plan."

"And make up with Mom, will you?"

"That's the plan, too."

Thirty minutes later, Stone stood on the screen porch and knocked on Holly's front door. She made him wait a long time before she answered, cracking the door open just enough to ask, "What do you want?"

"I was hoping we could talk."

"If I wanted to talk to you, I would have answered one of the five hundred times you called me this week." But she turned and walked away, leaving the door open, which Stone took as an invitation to enter.

As he closed the door behind him, Holly flopped down on the couch and curled her feet underneath her. There was a nearly empty bottle of wine on the coffee table with a half-full glass next to it. She wore denim shorts that weren't exactly Daisy Dukes but didn't reach all the way down to her knees either, and a tight white tank-top that clung to her chest. Her hair looked slightly damp, as if she had recently showered, but maybe it was just the heat and humidity.

Stone sat on the opposite end of the couch, set his Stetson down on the coffee table next to the wine bottle, and turned to face her. Now that he finally had the chance to say something to her, he didn't know where to start.

Before he could speak, she held up her hand. "Not one word about the wine, you hear me? I will not be judged in my own house."

"Yeah, because I'm such a judgy person," Stone said.

"Actually, you judge people all the time," Holly replied. "And then you usually kill them."

She must really be hurt, Stone thought. *She's cutting deep, going for the throat. And conveniently forgetting that she's killed people, too.*

He said, "That why you've been avoiding me? You don't want to be with someone whose body count is literal rather than figurative?"

"I'm avoiding you because you're still in love with your ex-wife."

"That's not true, and you know it."

"Don't tell me what I know," Holly snapped. "You literally said that if I wasn't in the picture, you would call Theresa back and see about giving your failed marriage another shot."

"That is *not* what I said," Stone replied. "I said I didn't know what I would do."

"Same thing."

"No, it's not."

She made a huffing noise.

"But none of that matters," Stone continued, "because

you *are* in the picture and you're the only woman I want to be with."

Holly looked at him, and though he couldn't be sure, Stone thought he saw the trace of tears in her eyes. "I want to believe you," she said. "I really do. But I just don't know if I can. There's still shit to figure out, Luke. For *both* of us. And I'm not sure either one of us can figure it out together. You know as well as I do that some journeys you have to take alone."

"Holly, I—"

She held up her hand to cut him off. "Don't, Luke. Just...don't."

He looked at her, wanting with every fiber of his being to make things right, but also knowing that pushing her right now would just drive her further away. So, he switched subjects and told her about his trip to Scar Lake.

"You think it's dangerous?" She seemed genuinely concerned.

"Three men missing in the span of a week, one of them an experienced mercenary?" Stone nodded. "Yeah, I'm guessing there's something dangerous going on up there."

"You need me to take care of Max and Rocky while you're gone?"

Stone shook his head. "No, I talked to Lizzy, and she's going to take care of them."

"So, what do you need from me?"

"If I'm not back in three days, I need you to call Braxx." Braxx was his best friend, a fellow warrior, his brother in blood, and they would go through hell for each other—*had* gone through hell for each other. "Tell him I'm in trouble and he'll be on the next train smoking to pull my ass out of the fire."

She stared at him, her eyes frank. "And what if you're already dead?"

"If I'm dead," Stone said grimly, standing up and clamping his Stetson back down on his head, "then God help whoever did it when Braxx gets his hands on them."

As he started to head for the door, Holly reached out and grabbed his hand. "Luke, take care of yourself out there. We may be having some problems at the moment, but that doesn't change the fact that I care about you, and I definitely don't want you dead."

He took a risk and leaned over to gently kiss her forehead. She didn't pull away, didn't resist, and he found some hope in that. "When I get back, we'll figure everything out," he said. "I promise."

She sighed, gave his hand a squeeze, and then let it go. "Just make sure you come back," she said.

EIGHTEEN

STONE MADE it to Scar Lake by early afternoon, when the sun had just crossed its zenith and the heat was just a few degrees away from scorching. There was no sign of the Donners' Jeep at the trailhead, but that didn't mean anything. If Mike and Carson had run afoul of dangerous individuals, then those individuals might very well have cleaned up their mess by making the Jeep disappear.

He strapped on his backpack, doused himself with insect repellent, traded his leather Stetson for a baseball cap, and headed up the trail with the Rossi Triple Black .30-30 in his hand, a round already levered into the chamber. He made his way across a rickety bridge that had definitely seen better days, passed a huge log stuck in the fork of a tree that reminded him of a teeter-totter, and hiked his way to Pastor Burke's cabin.

He found it empty. No gear at all. No sign the Donners had ever been there. Yeah, sure, maybe they had decided to go somewhere else without telling anybody, but it was just as possible that someone had stolen their stuff after dealing with Mike and Carson.

Keep looking. Don't jump to conclusions.

He stowed his own gear in the cabin—he'd called Burke on the drive up here and received permission to use the place as his operational base—and headed out into the woods.

He wasn't an expert tracker, but he had received training from the same Apache-blooded instructor who had taught him how to stalk and kill. And while the trail was several days old, it wasn't like the Donners had been trying to hide their tracks—nor Wade Garrett, for that matter—and Stone found the remains of Mike and the mercenary with relative ease.

Mike had clearly been dead longer, his body in worse shape from both decomposition and forest scavengers that had left large sections of skeleton visible through the putrefying flesh, but despite the damage, he was easy enough to identify. Birds had plucked away the soft tissue of his eyes and lips, but most of his facial structure remained intact, though partially rotted.

And the gaping head wound—axe or machete?—was clearly visible.

Looked like Mike Donner hadn't just gone missing. He'd been murdered.

And so had Wade Garrett.

The mercenary's body was in better shape, the scavengers not having been at it for as long as they had Mike Donner. The missing left hand and shattered kneecap proved the man had met a violent end, with the blown-open head putting a capper on the evidence.

Stone studied the bodies and wondered what the hell had happened. *Mike comes here and gets a blade to the skull. Garrett tracks him here and gets gunned down. What the hell is going on in these woods?*

And where the hell was Carson?

It took Stone nearly an hour to locate Carson's trail, but once he did, tracking was fairly easy. When he found a shattered walkie-talkie, his heart sank. Clearly, Carson was in trouble—or *had* been in trouble—as well.

Stone fought down the hopeless anger that wanted to hammer through his veins. He didn't have enough information to know whether Carson was dead or alive, but clearly, whoever was haunting these woods had no problem with killing. The two dead men back in the oak grove testified to that grim truth. Stone had to accept the possibility that this had evolved from a search-locate-rescue task into a mission of vengeance. Hell, even if he miraculously found Carson alive and was able to shepherd him to safety, Stone's deep belief in primal justice demanded payback against whoever had slaughtered Mike and Wade.

He scanned the ground for any sign of which direction Carson had gone. It didn't take long to find some old blood drops staining stones along a game trail, along with two sets of footprints in the mushy earth nearby. Was it Carson's blood, animal blood, or someone else's blood? Stone had no way of knowing. But he felt confident this was the trail Carson had taken. He moved stealthily through the thick brush, watching for more signs, alert for danger, his combat-honed sixth sense scanning in all directions for any threats.

Carson didn't know what to expect when his captors dragged him out of the dog kennel. All Honcho—the girl locked in the cage with him had explained her nicknames for the motley pack of organ harvesters—had said was,

"Time to tenderize the meat," and Goliath had opened the cage door, reached inside, and pulled him out as easily as a butcher grabbing a lamb for the slaughter. Carson kicked and fought, and while he was far from a weakling, his strength was no match for Goliath's freakish power and raw brutality.

"Leave him alone!" he heard the girl shout just before the giant's cinder-block fist crashed into his temple and sent him reeling into darkness.

When he regained consciousness, Carson found himself staring at the dirt, just inches below him. He was suspended face down in a spreadeagle position by thick ropes stretched taut between four wooden poles that pulled his arms and legs in all directions. The agony from his wrenched joints was excruciating, and his skull pounded with pain from the blow that had knocked him out. He coughed to clear his dry throat, not factoring in his close proximity to the ground, and a cloud of dirt slapped him in the face.

He strained to lift his head and saw Honcho, Patch, and Doc standing nearby, staring at him with bemused smiles on their faces.

"Time to play with the food," Patch smirked.

Is this the end? Carson wondered. *Am I about to die?*

Turning his head slightly, he saw Goliath hefting a heavy, ten-foot length of logging chain, the steel links coated with orange-brown rust. The sight did nothing to soothe Carson's nerves.

"Don't worry," Honcho said. "We're not gonna kill you. Not right now, anyway. That'll happen tomorrow, when our disgraced doctor here is ready to scoop out your innards. This right here? This is just a good flogging.

That rich idiot up in Canada likes his meat tenderized before we send it to him. I thought the bruising might cause problems, but the sick ol' son of a bitch says it actually improves the taste."

"Don't do this," Carson begged. "Please, man, don't do this."

"Look on the bright side, kid," Honcho said. "This time tomorrow, this will all be over and you get to see your mom again."

"Fuck you!"

"How utterly unoriginal. I hope you do better than that tomorrow when you come up with your last words before we slice you open and sell your guts to the highest bidder." Honcho gestured to Patch.

The one-eyed man walked toward Carson, plucking a knife from his belt.

Carson struggled against the ropes holding him, his punished joints screaming in painful protest. "Get away from me!" he yelled.

Patch ignored the frantic thrashing, and with a few deft strokes, slashed Carson's shirt away from his body, exposing his bare back to the hot afternoon air. Carson flinched every time he felt the cold steel graze his skin, but Patch possessed deft skill with the blade and the only thing the razored edge sliced was cloth. The skin on Carson's back remained untouched.

For now.

His knife work finished, Patch stepped back.

Carson fought against his bonds one more time. He knew it was useless, a waste of time and energy, but he couldn't just give up without a fight. He suffered no delusions—whatever was about to happen next would be bad —*real* bad.

Goliath hefted the rusty logging chain, and Carson felt his guts turn to water. The heavy chain coiled in the giant's fist like a medieval whip as he stepped behind his intended victim. Carson began to tremble, unable to control his fear, as Goliath prepared to scourge his helpless body. Despite Honcho promising not to kill him until tomorrow, Carson couldn't help but wonder if the heavy steel links would shatter his spine and send shards of vertebrae stabbing through his flesh.

Goliath raised the chain high as the other watched with savage glee.

Carson gritted his teeth. *Oh God, let this be over quick.*

The first blow lashed across his back and sent agony spasming through his body. The second blow felt like a sledgehammer pounding into the meat and muscle. He gritted his teeth, but the third strike slammed home and amplified the pain to breaking point.

Against his will, Carson screamed.

Stone froze when a man's agonized scream reverberated through the forest, wincing at the terrible pain in the cry. Somebody was going through a world of hurt right now. Could it be Carson? Maybe, but Stone had no way of being sure unless he put eyes on him, and even then, he'd only be going off an old photo of Carson that Mike had shown him.

Another scream echoed and faded, and Stone listened intently, doing his best to pinpoint the direction. Then he began to move again, running toward whatever threat awaited at the origin of those agonized cries.

He pushed through the thorns and bramble that scraped at him every step of the way as if nature itself was trying to slow him down. The going might have been easier if he slung the Rossi over his shoulder, but he refused to give up instant access to his rifle. The weight of the gun was reassuring, reminding him that he could react to whatever threat he encountered. He could fire a lever-action faster than most shooters could fire a semi-automatic, enabling him to dump a whole lot of lead downrange in just a few seconds.

He sprinted down the trail with less caution than usual, his boots occasionally slipping on muddy rocks. He told himself to be careful and not get hobbled by a twisted ankle as he bulled his way through the thorny brush.

Another scream shattered the afternoon air into hot splinters of aural agony.

Stone gritted his teeth and felt a cold, hard fist clench at his guts. He picked up the pace, sprinting toward those terrible cries. He knew that when he arrived, there was a damn good chance he would need to kill whoever or whatever was causing those cries.

And he knew that if killing needed to be done, he would do it without hesitation.

Inside the cabin, the woman in the cage stood and stared out the window as Carson suffered. This was hardly the first whipping she had witnessed, but this one hit her harder than most. Trapped in the dog kennel together for the last several days, she and Carson had grown close. Tears trickled down her filthy cheeks as the chain hit him again and again, and she whispered a prayer, "Please, God, make it stop. I can't take it. I can't take his screams. Make it stop. God, please, make it *stop*."

But the prayer went unanswered.

She tried not to let the darkness of hopelessness consume her. But it was so hard as she watched the chain lash across Carson's flesh.

Worse, she knew the flogging was just a prelude to his death.

Stone heard another cry of pain and gauged that the sound was coming from just over the nearby ridge. He ran up the slope and then dropped into a prone position. He could feel the adrenaline pulsing through him with every heartbeat as he slithered through the brush until he came to an opening in the large boulders that ringed the ridge. He found himself looking down into a crater-sized hollow.

What the hell is a cabin doing way back here?

He brought up the .30-30 and looked through the scope to assess the situation.

In just a matter of seconds, he took it all in.

The cabin. The half-buried skulls in the dirt. The four-man group, all of them armed, and Carson staked out on the ground, being whipped with a logging chain by an absolute giant.

He gritted his teeth and told himself not to be reckless. Reckless got you killed. But he sure as hell planned on rescuing that kid down there, and God help anyone who got in his way.

Stone watched as the giant brute raised the logging chain, hefting it as easily as a cowboy handles a bullwhip. Even through the scope, the savage glee was evident on the bestial behemoth's face.

Not on my fucking watch, Stone thought.

He quickly adjusted the crosshairs and squeezed the trigger.

The sound of the shot cracked through the air. The giant's right hand—the one holding the chain—was smashed by the bullet.

As the echo of the gunshot bounced between the boulders, the giant stared at his broken, bleeding hand as if wondering what the hell had just happened.

Stone raised his voice to a bellow and let it boom through the hollow. "Nobody move, or I'll kill every one of you sons of bitches!"

The man with the eyepatch apparently didn't believe in obeying orders. He immediately drew the revolver hanging on his hip and started to swing it toward Carson.

Stone slammed a round right through his chest, slightly left of center, tearing through his heart. The impact blasted the one-eyed man over backward, where he crashed heavily into the dirt. He went from alive to dead in just a few blood-spurting seconds.

"Anyone else want to try me?" Stone's voice held a hard, ruthless edge as he worked the lever-action, ejecting the spent casing and chambering a fresh cartridge.

One of the other men—the leader, apparently—clutched a shotgun but motioned for his two remaining companions to stay put and then asked, "What do you want?"

"The boy. Let him go."

"No." The leader's blunt refusal held a tone that indicated he believed his emphatic denial settled the matter.

Stone educated him with another shot from the rifle. The ground exploded less than a foot in front of the man, peppering his pants with dirt and debris. "Let's try this again," Stone said. "Release the boy. *Now.*"

He jacked the lever again, working the gun's action.

The leader made his move while Stone was halfway through the motion. The man moved with deceptive speed, his long strides covering a lot of ground in little time. Barely more than the blink of an eye, and the sawed-off shotgun was leveled against Carson's skull.

Stone quickly acquired the leader's head in the crosshairs. He could confidently drill a bullet through the man's brain. But doing so came with high risk: death spasms might cause a finger-twitch that pulled the shotgun's trigger and turned Carson's cranium into a gory jigsaw puzzle.

"Get your interloping ass down here, or I'll blow his goddamned head off," the leader warned. It didn't sound like he was bluffing.

"You pull that trigger, you're dead two seconds later," Stone promised. "And your buddies will be riding into hell right behind you."

Through the scope, he saw the man's finger tighten on the trigger, taking up the slack. "You do not want to mess with me, whoever you are," the man warned.

Stone seriously considered rolling the dice, taking the shot, and hoping for the best. If he did nothing, the twelve-gauge might snuff out Carson's young life. But if he put a bullet in the man's head, the twelve-gauge might still snuff out his life. It was a thorny predicament, one that made Stone uncharacteristically indecisive.

"Drop the fucking gun and come down here," the man yelled again.

"Let him go and then I'll come down." Damn straight it was a lie, but Stone figured it was for a good cause.

"Drop the gun and get your ass down here and then I'll release him." Apparently, the man with the shotgun had no problem lying either.

"This dance is getting old," Stone said. "Do what you gotta do, but I'm not letting go of this rifle until the boy is safe."

"Fine," the man replied. "You for him."

"What do you mean?"

"The boy goes free. You take his place."

Stone immediately thought of the Donners' tragic

history, how Mike Donner had been told by a masked madman to kill himself in order to save his wife and ultimately failed, playing the coward right in front of his son's eyes. Now, that son was the helpless victim, and Stone was being asked to sacrifice himself to save him. It was a choice he had no problem making, had he believed that the man would actually let Carson go free. But he knew there was no chance of that happening.

The man pressed the shotgun tighter against Carson's head. "I'm waiting."

Stone didn't say anything, weighing his options.

"Somebody's dying," the man growled. "You or him. Your choice."

"Let him go," Stone said. "I'll take his place." What the hell, one more lie wouldn't hurt anything.

"Toss the rifle and come down here first."

"Not a chance," Stone replied. "Not until Carson is safe. When I've decided he's far enough away, then I'll come down, and you can do whatever you want with me."

"How do I know you won't just start blasting once he's gone?"

"Guess you'll just have to trust me."

"Yeah, I'm not feeling that."

"I'm about out of patience," Stone said. "You don't start untying him, I'm just gonna start shooting and take my chances."

"Guarantee the kid won't survive that."

"Neither will you," Stone rasped. "So, what's it gonna be?"

The man held his ground, unflinching. Seconds ticked by without any movement. Stone reckoned his bluff was being called, and he would have to back up his tough words with hard action. The pad of his finger pressed tighter against the .30-30's trigger, getting ready to send hot death screaming down into the bone-strewn hollow. He prayed to God that Carson got out of this alive, but he was sure of one thing—no matter what happened in the next few moments, he was putting a bullet in the shotgunner's face.

But before he could start shooting, he felt the cold, hard barrel of a gun press against the back of his head.

NINETEEN

A GRUFF VOICE SAID, "Sorry to intrude, preacher, but I'm gonna need you to roll over real nice an' slow and don't even think about having a go at me with that stupid little thirty-thirty ya got there or I'll blast a blowhole where your head used to be."

Stone silently cursed—how the hell had someone snuck up on him?—and hesitated. Not like he had any options with a gun to his head, but instant compliance just wasn't in his genetic makeup.

The gruff voice said, "You're thinkin' bad thoughts, preacher man, the kind of thoughts that'll get the top of your spine blown out the front of your teeth. Now roll over, real slow like. Won't ask ya again."

Stone slowly obeyed, rolling onto his back, keeping his hands well away from his Rossie lever-action. He looked past the AR-15 rifle aimed at his face and focused on the man wielding it. Instant recognition. "Damn," he said. "You."

Rick nodded. "Ruff Rick's the name an' guns are my game," the sporting goods store owner said. "Kinda like the one I got right here. Converted to full-auto, by the way. Cut ya right in half at this range, so don't try no funny business, you read me, son?"

"I'm not your fucking son."

"Got a mouth on you for a preacher, don't ya? Heard that about ya." Rick chuckled. "Now let's take a little stroll down the hill, and you can meet my partners in crime."

"Partners?"

"That's what I said."

"What kind of sick business is this?" Stone asked.

"Funny you should mention *sick*," Rick replied. "Because sick people are what this business is all about."

"Care to elaborate?"

"Maybe later, if I'm in the mood. I'm sure you've got plenty of questions."

"Yeah," Stone said. "Starting with, how the hell did you get the jump on me? For the record, that's not easy to do."

"Lemme tell ya, son, I've been roamin' 'round these backwoods since before you were born, and I know every square inch of terrain better'n a teenage boy knows how to jerk his johnson. If I don't want ya to hear me comin', then ya won't."

Rick forced Stone to his feet and then marched him down into the hollow, the muzzle of the AR-15 never straying far from the middle of his back. He debated making a suicide play right then and there. Yeah, he would probably end up getting shot to hell, but something told him that whatever waited for him down at the cabin would be even worse than death by bullets.

But he decided to wait and hope that a better opportunity to turn the tables presented itself somewhere down the road.

The problem was, it looked like he was running out of road.

Deerflies buzzed their heads in the humid heat—Stone wanted to slap at them but knew that any sudden movement of his hands would earn him a bullet in the spine. Sure, he believed in heaven—and hell, for that matter—but he was in no hurry to get there. He just gritted his teeth and kept on going.

Just give me an opening.

He still couldn't believe someone had managed to sneak up behind him. Clearly, his combat-honed sixth sense had failed him. Desperate to save Carson, he had lost his focus during the verbal exchange with the shotgunner. Maybe he was finally losing his edge after all these years. The phrase *I'm getting too old for this shit* came to mind.

You're not that old, an internal voice said. *You got bested, that's all. It happens. You might be getting older, but you're not dead yet. So, stop whining, suck it up, and figure a way out of this mess.*

Stone glanced over his shoulder but found himself looking down the barrel of the rifle, the muzzle just inches from his nose.

"Keep lookin' straight ahead, preacher man, and don't even *think* about trying any shit," Rick warned. "Or I'll blow a brand-new hole where your fuckin' face used to be."

Stone saw that Rick's finger had taken up nearly all the trigger slack. It would only take another ounce or two of pressure to turn the man's harsh threat into gruesome reality. Stone defied the gun for a few tense heartbeats, staring defiantly into Rick's eyes. But when Rick's finger tensed on the trigger, Stone decided he wasn't ready to eat a bullet yet. He faced forward again and kept on walking down toward the cabin, like a condemned man marching to the execution chamber.

By the time they reached the bottom of the ridge, the

other men had untied Carson and dragged him inside the cabin. Clearly, they felt Rick had things well in hand. They left the dead man lying in the dirt. Maybe they planned on burying him later, after the sun went down and it wasn't so damn hot out.

Rick shoved Stone through the doorway so roughly that he stumbled over the threshold and nearly did a face plant on the floor. Rick followed him inside and said, "Look what I caught, gents."

The three men were hunkered around a table, the mildest-looking one working on stitching up the giant's hand that Stone had shot. It looked like the bullet had done plenty of damage. Stone took grim pleasure in knowing that, even if he died tonight, he had made the bastards bleed before they took him out. Maybe not the best mindset in which to meet his Maker, but he couldn't help the way he felt. His preacher side and warrior side were forever at odds within him, and right now, the warrior had the upper hand.

Upon seeing Stone, the giant immediately powered to his feet and used his good hand to reach for his hatchet. His eyes smoked with hatred like burning coals scorching his sockets.

"Put it away," Rick ordered. "Now's not the time. Why don't you go outside and bring in that hiker bitch so we can get to work on her. I'd say she's been hangin' long enough."

The giant continued to glare hot fury at Stone, but then did as commanded and lumbered out of the cabin.

Rick looked at the man who had held a shotgun to Carson's head and said, "Put him in the cage with the bitch an' the boy."

Stone was herded into a dog kennel, wondering if it would be his coffin. The door slammed shut behind him, and the padlock clicked into place. Carson was curled up in the corner, groaning softly in pain from the flogging he had suffered. He was still shirtless, his exposed back already darkening with bruises.

Stone knew he should be feeling some kind of hopelessness and alarm, but the only emotion he felt was total shock as he stared at the scarred woman trapped in the cage with him. But it was not the shock of revulsion—it was the shock of recognition. "I know you."

The woman nodded. "Yes, you do." Her voice was dry and coarse, as if rusty from lack of use, spilling over chapped, cracked lips. "I'm Jenny Burke. Pastor Burke's daughter."

"You're supposed to be dead."

"Well, I'm not dead, as you can see."

"Does your father know?"

"My father?" Jenny blinked, confused. "What are you talking about? My father's dead."

"No, he's not."

"Yes, he is. When these bastards took me, they killed him."

"No, they didn't."

"What?"

"He's alive," Stone said. "What made you think he was dead?"

"They told me they killed him." Jenny pointed at the three men sitting at the table who seemed to be listening to their conversation with bemusement. The giant had not come back yet.

Stone glanced at them, then fixed his eyes back on Jenny. "Guess that makes them liars, on top of whatever else they're doing here."

Jenny seemed to be struggling with the revelation that her father still lived. A myriad of different emotions played out on her face. "I've been here for a year. If he's alive, then why hasn't he come for me?"

Over at the table, Rick said, "I believe I can shed some light on that subject. You see, the reason Perry hasn't come for you is that, unlike *his* cowardly father"—Rick pointed at Carson—"Perry actually cares whether his family lives or dies, and he knows the second he tells anyone about us, your ass is deader'n a blind skunk tryin' to cross a six-lane highway during rush hour."

The giant chose that moment to crash through the door, carrying a woman's corpse over his shoulder. Her head was split in half, she was missing part of a leg, and her torso had been carved open like an autopsy incision.

What have I stumbled into? Stone wondered.

The body thumped as it was slammed down on the stainless-steel table.

Rick pushed back his chair. "Let's get outta the way and give the good doctor some room to work." He stood up and pointed at the man who had stitched up the giant's hand. "That's Doc, by the way," he said to Stone. "Not his real name, of course, but I'll be good an' damned if I'm gonna tell a sheriff the real names of my partners in crime, so we'll just stick to the nicknames that little lady in the cage with you gave them." He pointed at the giant. "That's Goliath, and the mean-lookin' feller with the shotgun is Honcho. The one-eyed jasper ya blasted outside was Patch. We'll probably just leave 'im for the coyotes."

"Should have blasted all you sons of bitches," Stone growled.

"You're absolutely right." Rick grinned. "You should've. And I'll bet you're really gonna regret not pullin' that trigger by the time Doc's done slicing ya open an' yankin' out yer guts."

Doc tossed Stone a wink and then buckled down to business. He donned a leather apron, picked up a knife, and began carving strips of flesh from the corpse, as indifferent as any butcher cutting up a cow or hog. The fact that it was a human body did not seem to bother Doc one single bit. The man's attitude seemed to be that meat was meat and bone was bone. Honcho fetched a large cooler, and Doc flipped hunks of flesh into it.

Dealing with some real sick sons of bitches here, Stone thought.

Rick continued to talk while Doc worked with the knife. "Perry knows that if he stops sending people our way, we'll kill his daughter instead. It's a supply an' demand kinda world. We make the demands, yer daddy is the supplier."

Jenny slipped her fingers between the links of the cage and gripped them tight enough to turn her knuckles white. Her face was just as pale. "What are you saying?"

"The day we snagged your perky little ass, instead of deep-sixing you and yer dear ol' dad right there on the spot, we struck a deal with him," Rick said. "A deal with the devil, so to speak. At least, I'm sure that's how he figured it. He shuffled on back to town an' told everyone you were dead. We even gave him a finger from another woman, a previous visitor, an' put your class ring on it to help sell the story."

Rick paused as Doc picked up a meat cleaver and chopped through a thick section of femur, then resumed talking. "Of course, that story was a bunch o' bullshit. Truth was, we kept you alive, and in return, Perry keeps sendin' people our way so we can harvest their organs. Every time someone mentions they'd like to go for a hike, commune with nature, he suggests here. Whenever a couple needs some alone time, he offers them his lodge. Every time some sissy-ass father and his derelict son need to bond, he suggests a little huntin' trip to Scar Lake. Ya gettin' the picture yet? Your daddy sends us lambs for the slaughter, and in return, we don't slaughter *his* precious little lamb."

Jenny looked horrified. "No, not my father...he'd never...*never* do something that evil. He couldn't."

"He could, he can, and he does," said Rick, as Doc put down the cleaver, picked up the knife again, and resumed methodically filleting meat from bone, tossing the morsels into the cooler. "You'd be surprised what someone will do to protect the ones they love."

Stone ignored the desecration of the body taking place right in front of him and asked, "Why do you do it?"

"Do what?"

"Kill people." Stone gestured at the ghastly tableau on the table. "Butcher them."

"Money, that's why," Rick replied. "Love to give you a more existential answer, but when ya boil it down to brass tacks, that's pretty much it. Cold, hard cash. People pay a lot—and I do mean *a lot*—of money—for black market organs. When yer lookin' death in the face while yer on some miles-long waitin' list tryin' to get a liver transplant, your morals go out the window and yer ready to spend a fortune. We cater to those people in need an' make a boatload of cash doin' it."

"People in need." Stone snorted. "Let's not pretend you're saints. You're fucking murderers."

Rick said, "Lemme tell ya something, preacher. There are over a hundred thousand people on the transplant list in the United States, and another five thousand or so in Canada. When yer lookin' the Reaper in the face and somebody like me comes along and offers you a chance at life, at salvation...well, to that person, I look an awful lot like a fuckin' saint, you can bet yer ass."

"Is there a problem? Damn straight there is," Stone said. "But killing the innocent to save the sick isn't the answer. You're nothing but a predator, preying on the desperate and murdering for profit."

"You're sounding a might holier-than-thou for a preacher, or sheriff, or whatever you wanna call yourself, who's gunned down a whole mess of people since you rode into town." Rick gestured around the room at his partners. "Looks like we're not the only killers around here."

"And I'll do it again, if they got it coming," Stone said. "Fact is, you should kill me, because if you don't, I'm going to kill you."

"Oh, don't worry." Rick chuckled. "We're gonna kill you, all right. You'll be in next week's shipment. Organs to the highest bidder, meat to some stupid-rich, crazy clown up in Canada who thinks eatin' human flesh makes ya live longer. Says the victims are called *long pigs* in the cannibal subculture, if you can believe that. Guess it's Polynesian in origin or some shit." Rick shrugged. "All I know is he pays a fortune for the meat and claims he's a hundred and twenty years old."

"That's bullshit, and you know it. The guy's blowing smoke up your ass."

"Oh, I don't believe it," Rick said. "But hey, it's no less bullshit than your Bible-buddies who go to church every Sunday, suck down a communion wafer an' a shot of wine, and believe it magically transforms into the actual flesh an' blood of Christ Himself." He shrugged. "Guess you morons only believe cannibalism is okay if yer in a church and eatin' God."

"I'm not Catholic," Stone replied.

Doc continued to work, his blades crimsoned. The tip of his tongue protruded from his mouth in concentration as he toiled.

"Not my place to judge where someone tries to find eternal life," Rick said. "You can believe in an invisible man in the sky, or you can believe chowin' down on some long pig will do the trick. Makes no difference to me. But at least the long pigs make me money."

"You're gonna find out that money doesn't spend in hell," Stone rasped.

"Oh, you gonna send me there?"

"First chance I get."

"Well, then, guess it's a good thing for me that yer never gonna get a chance."

"God got Daniel out of the lion's den. He got the three Hebrew children out of the fiery furnace. I'm willing to bet He can get me out of this dog cage to kill your sick ass."

Doc had finished cutting all the flesh from the bone. Little remained of the female hiker other than a dripping skeleton with clusters of gristle. Rick reached over with his foot, kicked the cooler lid shut, and gave Stone a wicked grin. "Sorry to tell ya this, preacher, but there ain't no God here."

TWENTY

STONE, Carson, and Jenny remained in the cage for the next several hours. Rick and his gang brought in another corpse, this one male—Jenny explained it was the husband of the first woman—and stripped that one down to the bone too, making Stone wonder just how much human flesh the sick-brained billionaire in Canada could eat. Then the organ harvesters cracked open bottles of beer and started drinking. Evening became night, and the sun replaced the moon, as they guzzled down the booze, except for Goliath.

While the others drank, he just stared at Stone and used his good hand to play with his hatchet, slowly and methodically running his thumb along the honed edge to test its sharpness. The beauty of a hatchet, Stone thought, was that you could wield it with just one hand. Then again, Goliath was big enough that he probably could have wielded a full-size medieval battle axe one-handed.

Sitting with his back against the side of the dog kennel, arms draped loosely over his knees, Stone stared back at the giant. "See something you like, big guy?"

Goliath growled, "See something I'd like to tear apart.

Thinking about ripping off your arms and legs and shoving them up your ass sideways."

"Stop thinking about it and let's see what you got."

Rick drained a bottle of beer, belched, and said, "Careful there, Goliath. Pastor Stone here is a genuine badass. A two-fisted, gunslinging, ass-kicking hellraiser with a serious body count."

"We looking at the same piece of shit? Because I see a guy I could break in half in about two seconds flat, even with one hand all shot up."

Stone said, "Why don't you stop flapping your lips like some kind of two-bit pussy and put your money where your mouth is?"

"Yeah, speaking of mouths, I think I've had just about enough of yours." Goliath slammed his good fist down on the table and then pointed at Stone. "Me and you, preacher boy. Time to find out who the tougher SOB is—the man of God or the man of the devil."

Rick rolled his eyes. "Fine. Go drag him outta the cage and get it over with." He let out a long-suffering sigh. "Never figured out why boys need to play the whose-dick-is-bigger game, but let's get it outta your systems."

As Goliath stepped toward the kennel, Stone hid a cold smile. He'd successfully goaded the big brute into letting him out of this cage, and that was the first step toward escape. Of course, the next step was the hard one—winning the fight against this mountain of a man. Stone couldn't remember ever facing an opponent as humongous as Goliath. The man's fist and feet would hit like 40-pound sledgehammers.

So don't get hit, he told himself.

Yeah, easier said than done.

As Stone stepped out of the cage, he glanced at his Rossi .30-30 rifle leaning against the wall near the table.

Rick caught the look. "Thinkin' 'bout goin' for it,

preacher? Thinkin' that if ya can just get yer hands on that piece of hot lead hardware, ya might be able to save yer skin, avenge all the killings, and save the boy an' the girl? That the general idea flittin' through yer little peabrain right now?"

"Nah." Stone shook his head and sized up Goliath. "Just thinking about how bad I'm gonna fuck up this big bastard."

"Well, you can think about that all ya want, but for those thoughts to become reality would take a miracle, the likes of which ain't been seen since the loaves an' fishes." Rick chuckled. "And in case you ain't noticed, God hasn't exactly been making His presence felt around here in quite some time."

"Got a newsflash for you," Stone replied. "God's always there, even in hell."

The last word came out in a gasp, the breath knocked out of him when Goliath slammed a fist into his stomach. Stone hadn't even seen the blow coming. The guy moved faster than any big man Stone had ever squared off against.

Goliath hauled back and fired another punch that crashed into his ribcage like a cement block. Stone managed to twist away so he didn't take a direct hit that would break bones, but it still hurt like a son of a bitch. He staggered back, sucking air from the first blow, wincing from the second blow, retreating from the human wrecking ball he now faced.

Goliath advanced, hunting him down, his face an ugly mask of violent satisfaction as he realized he might very well decimate his opponent. "Thought you were hot shit?" he taunted.

"You score a couple love taps and think it's game over?" Stone scoffed. "This dance is just getting started, big boy."

Goliath stalked forward, pushing ahead with ruthless momentum. His fist lashed out, and Stone took a shot to the temple. He couldn't believe the giant's speed.

As Stone rocked to the side and tried to shake the cobwebs out of his head, he remembered a hand-to-hand combat instructor telling him, *"There's always somebody bigger out there. There's always somebody faster. There's no way you can win every fight. Best you can do is try to win most of them."*

Yeah, well, now he had run into someone bigger *and* faster.

And there was a pretty good chance he was about to take a loss.

But he wasn't going down without a fight.

He ducked beneath Goliath's next swing and cranked a punch into the giant's gut, putting all his power behind it. The solid strike would have incapacitated most men, but Goliath didn't even flinch. The jarring impact vibrated up Stone's arm and into his shoulder. It felt like he had bruised his knuckles on the steel slabs that were the man's abdominal muscles. He might as well have punched the armored plates of an M-1 Abrams tank.

Stone quickly rose out of the crouch and slammed a looping punch into Goliath's jaw. The blow didn't do a damn thing. The giant's head barely moved.

Goliath grinned at him. "That all you got, boy?"

Yeah, actually, Stone thought.

Goliath's elbow snapped down across Stone's shoulder like a guillotine blade with enough force to nearly crack the collarbone. Pain blazed through his chest, and he stumbled back, trying to come to terms with the fact that he was getting the crap kicked out of him. He couldn't even remember the last time he had lost a fight.

I'm getting old. Slipping in my old age. I've beaten guys who are big and fast before.

He refused to let fear poison his mind. This was just another fight, he tried to tell himself. Just another fight like the hundreds, maybe even thousands, he had been in before. He needed to let his training take over and put this clown down for the count.

He circled, seeking an opening, ignoring the taunts from Rick, Honcho, and Doc, as well as the calls of encouragement from Jenny in the cage. He focused on the battle, looking for an opening, a way to defeat Goliath's gargantuan strength and shocking speed. Every fighter had a weakness. You just had to find it.

Stone was fast in his own right. He faked one way, then went the other, sliding behind Goliath. He reached up and snaked his arm around the giant's thick neck, gripping him in a chokehold like a python trying to crush and kill. For the first time since the fight had started, Stone felt a semblance of control. Maybe he could beat this bastard after all.

And then Goliath bent at the waist, leaned forward, and hurled Stone over his back like he was nothing more than a bag full of cotton balls.

Stone hit the ground hard, spine hammering against the wooden floor, dust exploding around him. Pain spiked through him, and he rolled onto his side, coughing, sucking air like he was drowning.

I'm gonna lose. The thought cut through him like a cold knife. *I'm gonna lose, and we're all gonna die.*

He dragged in another breath and told himself to keep fighting. He had been in bad spots before and always found a way to come out on top.

Goliath loomed over him, blocking out the light. Stone tried to roll away, but a swift boot to the ribs put an end to that play, flipping him over on his back again. Another kick cracked across his jaw, and he saw stars.

With his bell soundly rung, Stone mounted little defense when Goliath reached down, grabbed him by the shirt, and dragged him to his feet like a rag doll. The few ineffectual blows he managed—desperate, wild—bounced off the giant as if they were nothing more than vapor. The big brute absorbed them with no visible effect. Stone might as well have hurled feathers at the guy.

Goliath hauled off and delivered a brutal cross punch that detonated against Stone's already bruised jaw. He felt his knees buckle, and the world went silent. He was falling backward, and it felt like he was in slow motion, like gravity didn't want to finish the job. But then reality kicked back into high gear, and the floor rushed up to meet him.

He struggled to stay conscious, the darkness crowding the edge of his vision as his beaten body tried to shut down. He felt himself lifted into the air as Goliath picked him up and then slammed him down on the table, with the hoots and hollers of the rest of the gang urging him on. His head hit so hard that it felt like his skull had split open. The darkness crept even further into his eyesight. He managed to throw a punch but it might as well have come from a burlap scarecrow for all the good it did.

Even with one hand out of commission, the giant's freakish strength enabled him to hold Stone down with relative ease. Stone landed a few more weak punches, but it felt like punching a concrete block with a dandelion.

He heard Jenny scream, "Leave him alone!" and turned his head to see her pressed against the wall of the kennel, her fingers curled through the links, knuckles white.

When he turned his head back, Goliath leaned down

and pressed his right forearm against Stone's throat, pinning him to the table. With his good hand, the giant snatched up a beer bottle and smashed it to pieces on the table next to Stone's head. He then picked up a slender, needle-like shard.

"Open up and say *ahhhh,* motherfucker."

Stone didn't panic, but a cold chill crawled through his guts at the thought of having broken glass shoved in his mouth. He clenched his jaw so tightly that he risked cracking a tooth. Better a ruptured molar than a shard down his throat.

Stone dug deep and summoned another reserve of defiant strength. He brought his knee up, quick and hard, connecting with Goliath's ribs. He did it three more times in rapid succession, striking the same spot again and again, hoping to hear the wet crack of snapping bone. God, he wanted to hurt this son of a bitch so badly. The giant winced, grunted, and took a half step back, the first sign of pain he had shown. His forearm loosened against Stone's neck.

Stone knew he might never get a better chance.

Please, God, let me kill this bastard.

Not the most righteous prayer, but he didn't care.

Stone reached out, grabbed a shard out of the pile next to his head, and lunged up, slashing the jagged edge across Goliath's right eye. No mercy, no hesitation. The glass blade cut the eyeball wide open, and Goliath staggered back, screeching, as bloody fluid spurted from the popped pupil.

The rest of the criminal clan froze for a moment, unable to believe what had just happened. Then Jenny pounded her fist against the cage and yelled, "Oh, yeah!" and they all burst into frenzied motion.

Snarling in pain, Goliath managed to claw the hatchet out of its sheath and swing it at Stone. But he was already in motion, rolling off the table, forcing his punished body to move as fast as possible. The hatchet thudded into the table, narrowly missing him, punching through the stainless steel.

Stone moved with the focus and speed that comes from knowing you are truly screwed if you're too slow. He managed to grab the Rossi .30-30 leaning against the wall before anyone could stop him. He pivoted toward Goliath just as the giant pulled the hatchet back for another swing.

Stone hit the trigger and drilled a bullet into Goliath's gut. The behemoth staggered backward, dropped the hatchet, and clutched at the oozing hole in his belly. But damn if the guy didn't stay on his feet.

Somewhere along the way, Doc had acquired the .357 Magnum that Patch had carried before he died. The disgraced surgeon started to swing the weapon toward Stone's position. He clearly wasn't a gun guy, because he held the heavy revolver with awkward unfamiliarity.

Stone, on the other hand, was definitely a gun guy. Nothing awkward about the shot he hammered into the doctor's head. The bullet cored a gaping tunnel through the man's skull and exited the back, hurling bloody chunks of bone everywhere.

Rick's hand was on his AR-15, and Honcho was trying to bring his sawed-off shotgun into play as Doc's brain-sludge splattered the wall.

Stone leveled the .30-30 at them. "Don't even think about it, shitheads." His body ached from the beating Goliath had administered, but steely resolution mixed with adrenaline kept the pain from crippling him. "Drop the guns."

Rick and Honcho both stopped in their tracks and let their rifles fall to the floor at their feet. Still, Rick didn't seem all that concerned about having a gun pointed at him. "In case you can't count, preacher," he said, "you've only got one shot left and there's two of us. Three, if ya count Goliath over there, who ain't exactly down for the count yet, in case ya haven't noticed."

He wasn't wrong. The Rossi lever-action only held six shots, and between the shots fired from the ridge and the ones fired just now, Stone knew only a single bullet remained in the gun.

He shifted the muzzle so it was aimed directly at Honcho. "So I'll put a slug through his ugly face,"—he said, then swung the Rossie toward Rick—"and then I'll just shove this rifle up your ass. As for big boy over there, I'm betting with a bullet in his guts, I can take him now."

"Or you can just put the gun down and maybe, just maybe, I'll think about lettin' you walk outta here alive," said Rick.

"I like my plan better," Stone said. "Let Jenny and Carson out of that cage, and everyone gets to live to die another day."

Rick shook his head. "Ain't gonna happen."

"Then you're dead. Simple as that."

"Soon as you pull that trigger, Honcho here will have that sawed-off in play an' cut you in half quick as shit."

"Maybe. But you'll still be dead."

Rick cocked his head and studied Stone. "You're tellin' the truth, ain't ya, preacher? I can see it in yer eyes, plain as day. You're in a killin' mood."

"You sick bastards butcher people and sell their organs. Doesn't exactly take a genius to figure out why I might want to blow your brains out your ass," Stone rasped. "But what I want right now is for you to let Jenny and Carson out of that damn cage."

Rick turned to Honcho and said, "Do it," before turning back to Stone. "Ya won't get far. Ya know that, right? These are our hills, our woods. We'll hunt you down in the dark, and when we get you back, what we do to ya next will make that beating ya just took look like a fuckin' pillow fight."

"Making threats right now might be hazardous to your health." Stone kept his finger tight on the trigger. He really wanted to blast a hole through Rick's face. If he had two bullets left instead of just one, he'd probably be doing just that.

Honcho walked over to the kennel, undid the padlock, and opened the door.

"Now back away," Stone ordered.

Honcho complied, but his angry glare made it clear that if he ever got his hands on Stone, there would be no mercy. Stone had no problem with that. The feeling was mutual.

Jenny stared at the open door for a moment, as if unable to believe what was happening. She probably felt like a damned soul who has suddenly found an escape hatch out of hell but is too afraid to take it for fear it might just be an illusion designed to give birth to hope... and then brutally crush it.

Stone was just starting to think she really wasn't going to leave the cage when she suddenly turned to Carson and helped him climb to his feet and exit their prison.

Goliath, leaning against the wall, made a growling sound as they ducked out of the kennel, his remaining eye blazing hotly. Stone couldn't believe the giant was still on his feet. He acted like he had nothing more than a stomach cramp instead of a close-range gut-shot. He looked like he just needed a short breather and then he'd be ready to go another couple rounds.

If the Rossi had been fully loaded, Stone probably would have put a bullet in the brute's forehead, just to be sure he was down for the count.

"Well, well, well," Rick sneered. "A coward's son, a beat-to-hell preacher, and a useless little whore. Won't exactly be the most challenging hunt we've ever been on."

Stone heard Jenny open the cabin door behind him. He began backing toward it, keeping the rifle trained on the organ harvesters. "I'd think long and hard about that hunt if I were you."

"Yeah, well, you ain't me," Rick said.

Stone paused in the doorway. "Just remember, sometimes the hunter is the one who gets killed."

He kicked the door shut, and he, Jenny, and Carson fled into the night.

TWENTY-ONE

THEY RAN TOWARD THE WOODS, knowing that at any moment, Rick and Honcho would be after them like hounds chasing hares. As they passed the body of Patch still lying dead in the dirt, Stone paused just long enough for a quick pat-down, finding a folding knife in the man's pocket. He shoved it into his own pocket as they hustled up the ridge, passed the huge boulders, and entered the thick, unforgiving forest.

"What's our plan?" Jenny asked, panting. Just the short dash across the hollow and up the ridge had left her nearly out of breath. Not a good sign.

"Right now, the plan is to run like hell," Stone said.

"Good plan," said Carson. He was clearly hurting from the whipping he'd endured, but appeared to be powering through the pain. Stone could relate, because that was pretty much what he was doing himself.

They moved through the woods at a fast trot, ignoring the limbs that scourged them and the thorns that scratched them and the roots that stumbled them. More accustomed to moving through the dark in dangerous environments, Stone fared better than the two teenagers.

It soon became apparent that Jenny could not maintain the quick pace. She tried her best, but after a few minutes of loping through the dark woods, she collapsed against a tree, heaving for air like an asthmatic having an attack. Her fingers dug into the bark as she grimaced in pain.

Stone turned around and came back to her, touching her lightly on the shoulder. "Are you okay?"

She shook her head, still trying to catch her breath. Finally, she said, "Have to…rest. Been in that…cage…a long time. No…exercise." The words came out in staggered huffs. "Lungs…aren't…what they…used to be."

"Stopping isn't really an option," Carson, standing nearby, said. "Those guys can't be far behind us."

Stone nodded and scanned their surroundings, but all he could see was moonlit darkness and twisted shadows.

"Sorry…no choice. Have to…rest." Jenny looked at them. "Leave me…if you have to." Her eyes were luminous in the moonlight.

Carson stepped forward and gently touched her cheek. "That's never going to happen," he said.

Even Stone could feel the connection between the two of them. It made him think of Holly, but he refused to let that thought linger and distract him from the task at hand—survival. He let the two teenagers have a few tender moments and tried not to think of those moments as a waste of time. Besides, as Carson and Jenny stared into each other's eyes, a plan started to form in Stone's mind.

Sometimes you had to use bait to take down a predator.

Carson and Jenny concealed themselves behind a large cluster of fallen, decaying logs with giant white mushrooms sprouting all over them. Stone had left them the lever-action rifle with its one remaining shot in case the plan failed, though Carson doubted a single bullet would be enough to save them if Stone's plan didn't work. Still, he'd rather have the rifle than the folding knife that was the preacher's only weapon.

Cut their fucking hearts out, Stone, he thought. *Make them pay for what they did to my dad, to those poor hikers, to everyone they butchered.*

Watching the trail through gaps in the piled logs, he asked Jenny, "Hey, since you're a pastor's kid, do you still believe in prayer?"

He expected her to hesitate—how could she not, given all she had been through?—but she answered immediately. "Yes. Why?"

"Because you might want to fire one off right now."

"Something wrong with your lips?"

Carson glanced at her. "Between the dead mom and now the dead dad, guess I'm just not much into God these days. Kind of surprised you are, truth be told, after all the shit you've been through."

"How do you think I got through all that shit?"

Carson stared at her for a moment, impressed by her unshakable faith. Abducted, tortured, violated, and yet she still continued to believe. He wouldn't have been surprised if she told him that her favorite Bible verse was, *Though He slay me, yet will I trust Him.*

He shook his head and said to her, "Just so you and I are clear, if we make it out of this alive, I'm going to kill your father."

"If we make it out of this alive," Jenny replied, "I'm going to ask you not to."

"My dad is dead because of him, along with a whole lot of other people he sent here to be slaughtered. We should just let him get away with that?" Carson shook his head. "Sorry, but I don't think I can do that."

Jenny didn't respond. Probably realized that nothing she said would change his mind.

He peered into the darkness, grip tight on the rifle. The moon glowed like the bloated belly of a corpse in the stygian sky. "You have a problem with killing these pricks that are after us?" he asked.

Jenny shook her head. "I think we're a little past turning the other cheek."

"Good," Carson replied. "Because I'll tear their heads off with my bare hands if I get a chance."

Stone had retreated back down the trail about fifty yards, hoping to ambush anyone following them. He had no doubt that Rick or Honcho or both of them would give chase. Given the evil the men had committed, they couldn't just sit back and let their prisoners escape back to civilization to tell their story. No, they would come, they would hunt and pursue, and Stone planned to intercept them.

The night would have been black as the devil's soul if not for the moonlight cutting through the darkness. Concealed in the brush, Stone waited and listened, his senses probing the silence. There was nothing complicated about his plan. The teenagers crouched behind the fallen logs up ahead were the bait. Stone just needed to take down the predator—or predators—before the kids became fallen prey.

It wasn't long before he heard twigs snapping and leaves crackling as something heavy stomped through the woods with all the grace of a pissed off grizzly. Stone felt his muscles tense, preparing for action. The folding knife he had pilfered from the dead man's pocket was already open, four-inch blade ready to strike and cut. It wasn't much, but Stone had killed with far less. He breathed shallowly, not wanting to betray his position. For this to work, timing was everything.

Crouched low and concealed in a thick tangle of brush, he watched and listened as the heavy footsteps pounded closer. A moment later, the maker of those footsteps stopped in a patch of silvery moonlight, and Stone felt a moment of surprise when he saw that it was Goliath. With a mangled hand, slashed eye, and a bullet in his guts, Stone had expected the hulking brute to be out of the fight.

Then again, he had seen men barely half Goliath's size shot all to hell who had somehow kept going, continued fighting, surviving on stubbornness, adrenaline, and raw stubbornness. Stone usually chalked it up to the grittiness of a warrior, the bone-deep refusal to surrender, but clearly it could apply to freakishly huge murderers as well. The look on Goliath's moonlight-scoured face was one of pure, unadulterated hatred. The burning, all-consuming desire to kill Stone was the reason the monster didn't just lie down and die. Stone almost admired the man's willpower.

But instead of admiring him, he planned to kill him.

Goliath seemed to ignore all the pain he must have been enduring. He clutched his hatchet and peered into the darkness with his remaining eye, searching for his prey, for the man who had hurt him, for the teenagers that had escaped his torturous grasp.

The giant took another step forward, moving out of the patch of moonlight and back into the dark shadows.

Now! Stone thought, hoping Carson had been watching and knew it was time to act.

As if on cue, Jenny bolted from the pile of logs, letting

out a loud cry as she fled from cover like a flushed rabbit. Carson was right behind her, and Stone could almost hear their thoughts. *Come on, you big bastard, take the bait.*

Goliath bellowed with rage and lunged forward with his hatchet raised. "Come here, you little shits!" he snarled as he passed Stone's position, seemingly oblivious to the threat lying in wait.

Stone emerged from the thicket with the stealth of a stalking panther and crept up behind the murderous giant. His body ached from the beating he had taken, but it wasn't vengeance that fueled his quest to kill. Right now, all he cared about was protecting the two teenagers he found himself in charge of.

He almost underestimated Goliath's speed and combat skills again. The giant seemed to possess a warrior's sixth sense. As Stone stalked up behind him, Goliath suddenly swung his hatchet backward without even turning around, the weapon moving in a deadly blur. Stone almost caught it right in the kisser. Only his own speed and agility saved him from getting his face split in half. He ducked under the blade at the last possible nanosecond and felt a few hairs shaved off his head.

Damn, that was close.

Powered by adrenaline, he rose up and rammed the knife into the side of Goliath's neck, just under his ear. The blade sliced through flesh and cartilage as it punched in all the way to the hilt. He twisted the knife as he pulled it out, tearing open the wound, and blood gushed everywhere. Goliath howled in surprise and pain and dropped the hatchet, slapping at the wound with his good hand to staunch the crimson flow. It didn't do much good.

He spun around to face his attacker.

Stone stabbed the blade into the hollow of the man's

throat with every bit of strength he had left. More blood gushed everywhere, splattering him with scarlet gore.

Goliath staggered backward, his good hand pressed to the side of his neck, his bad hand pressed against the frothing hole in his throat. His ankle caught on an exposed root, and he toppled to the ground like a chain-sawed oak. He twitched and writhed and gurgled for a bit and then finally went still.

Stone stared down at the giant corpse, surveying all the various wounds Goliath had soaked up before finally giving up the ghost. As Carson and Jenny walked over, he shook his head and muttered, "Talk about one hard-to-kill son of a bitch."

Jenny stared distastefully at the body, no doubt haunted by memories of what the man had done to her, not to mention all the others he had murdered. "Are you sure he's dead?" she asked.

Carson picked up Goliath's hatchet and slammed it into the top of the giant's skull.

"We are now," he said.

Stone wiped the blood from his knife, folded it up, and put it back in his pocket.

Carson suddenly jerked the hatchet out of Goliath's cranium and exploded into a berserker rage. With hysterical frenzy, he swung the weapon again and again and again, hacking and slicing and chopping at the body. "Die!" he screamed as sharp steel thudded into dead flesh. "You piece of shit! You killed my father! Die! Die! Die!"

When the corpse was little more than butchered meat, he stopped chopping, sleeved blood and sweat from his face, and stared at Stone as if daring him to say something critical.

But all Stone said was, "You done?"

"That fucking asshole deserved to die."

"No argument from me." Stone glanced back in the direction of the cabin. "There's still two of them left, so we need to keep moving. If we can make it back to my truck, we can get the hell out of here."

Stone led them through the woods, not running, not walking, but a pace somewhere in between, which was about as fast as the terrain would allow, especially for someone experiencing shortness of breath like Jenny.

They had gone several hundred yards when Jenny asked, "Do you still have the keys to your truck?"

"No."

"Then how do you plan on starting it?"

"It's an old truck. Easy enough to hotwire."

"I can do that," Carson said. "Learned a few tricks in juvie. How to use toothpaste to cut through steel bars. How to make a shank out of toilet paper. How to make sure you never drop the soap in the shower. And oh yeah, how to hotwire a car. All we have to do is make it there in one piece."

"Easier said than done," Jenny said.

"We'll make it," Carson replied, putting a hand on her shoulder. The other hand still held the bloody hatchet. "I promise."

Stone almost told him not to make a promise he might not be able to keep, but decided against it. He could tell by the way their eyes met and lingered that there was definitely an attraction between the two teens. Maybe an attraction spawned from the hell of mutual trauma, but attraction nevertheless, and sometimes shared pain knitted two souls together more tightly than anything else. He had seen it before, and even though his and Holly's romance had not followed that particular trajectory, seeing the two teenagers gaze at each other reminded him of her. He tried not to think about the fractures in their relationship. Their love might have taken a hit, but it was just a bruise, not a fatal blow.

At least, that's what he told himself.

He just needed to get out of here alive and find out if it was true.

TWENTY-TWO

A QUARTER MILE behind his prey, Honcho stumbled upon Goliath's chopped-to-hell remains. The bloody mess was kind of hard to miss, strewn across the trail. He canted the sawed-off shotgun over his shoulder as he stared down at his partner—or rather, what was left of his partner—for a few moments.

His face remained expressionless. Had anyone been watching, they would not have seen even a flicker of emotion. He and Goliath—God, the girl's stupid nicknames really had stuck—had been part of the black-market organ harvesting ring together for a couple years, but he would hardly have called the hulking giant his buddy. Greed and murder were not exactly the best foundations on which to form a meaningful friendship.

No, he didn't feel much sense of loss. Mostly just anger that Stone was putting the boots to their whole bloody business. But Rick had orchestrated the whole operation, and as long as he and Rick were still alive, they could always start back up somewhere else. The distribution network remained intact and would no doubt continue to do business with them if they could pull the pieces back together.

But that only worked if Stone, the boy, and the bitch didn't make it back to civilization and blow the whole thing wide open.

He stepped around the butchered corpse and studied the ground beyond. You didn't need to be an expert tracker to see which way Stone, Carson, and Jenny had fled. The scuffed dirt, overturned leaves, and broken underbrush were practically neon signs glowing in the night if you knew what to look for.

Shotgun in hand, Honcho continued his hunt.

Jenny was definitely out of shape, but Stone couldn't hold that against her. Kind of hard to maintain a good exercise regimen when you're locked up in a dog cage. When she started lagging again, Carson took her hand and practically dragged her behind him.

"Just leave me," she said more than once.

And every time she said it, Stone replied, "Not a chance."

The forest was not their friend. Stone had encountered worse terrain during his warrior days—the Darien Gap came to mind—but not by much. Thick, brushed closed in on them like the sides of a living coffin. Thorns reached out to snag their clothes and slow them down, piercing through to the skin. Roots rose up to cause them to trip and stumble. Limbs whipped their faces. Stone held up better than the two teenagers, who were having a rough go of it. But he noticed that no matter what happened, Carson never let go of Jenny's hand.

Until the young man tripped over a bear trap.

Carson twisted as he fell, so he landed on his back, his

arms reaching out to cushion Jenny's fall. She landed on top of him so they were chest to chest, their faces just inches apart. It might have turned into a tender moment if they both hadn't spotted a woman's severed leg lying just a few feet away from them.

Jenny gasped and rolled away. Carson jumped to his feet and pulled her up.

Stone examined the scene for a moment and then handed Carson the rifle. "Hold this."

Carson accepted the weapon. "What are you doing?"

"I've got an idea." Stone picked up the bear trap and slung it over his shoulder by the chain. He did his best to keep the metal from clanking, but total silence was impossible, and sound carried easily through the night air. It was quite possible their pursuers could hear them. But it didn't really matter, because the trail they were leaving through the woods wouldn't require much skill to follow. Stone might have been able to navigate the unforgiving terrain without leaving much spoor to track, but the two teenagers didn't possess his skills.

"Care to explain your idea?" Jenny asked.

"Just going to leave a little surprise for our friends," Stone replied.

Stone carried the bear trap all the way to the teeter-totter. He figured he could have made it in less than thirty minutes if he had been alone, but with Jenny slowing them down, it took the better part of an hour. Sixty long, tense minutes of not knowing if or when their tormentors would pounce out of the shadows. Dawn was hours away, and darkness still blanketed the woods.

They stopped just once, at the Burke cabin. Stone hoped to find his gear still inside so he could grab more cartridges for the .30-30. But everything was gone, no doubt stolen by the organ harvesters. They seemed pretty efficient at wiping out all traces of anyone who showed up at the cabin and ended up on their butchering table.

That meant he still just had the one shot left in the rifle.

And two men still hunting them down.

If possible, he needed to save that bullet for the last man.

They exited the cabin and made it the rest of the way to the teeter-totter without incident. Maybe they would get lucky and Honcho and/or Rick wouldn't find them, but Stone wasn't a big fan of relying on luck. He preferred to tip the odds in his favor whenever possible.

He quickly set up his trap. A bit of a long shot that it would actually work, but it was worth a try. If whoever came up the trail after them didn't fall for it, then no harm, no foul, just a couple minutes wasted. But if things went the way he hoped, one of their pursuers would be slowed down, possibly even taken out of commission for good.

Thoroughly winded, Jenny didn't help much, but Carson pitched in once Stone explained his plan. "I'm glad I'm not facing those bastards alone," the young man said as they worked.

Stone gave him a tight nod. Carson had been through hell, but he clearly still had some fight left in him.

With the site prepped and the trap laid, Stone, Carson, and Jenny kept moving down the path, trying to reach the parking lot before anyone caught up to them.

Honcho moved silently. He could hear his prey not far up

ahead. The girl's panting gave them away. The pretty little bitch was clearly out of shape. No big surprise there.

He cut through the patches of moonlight that dappled the trail, pausing in one of the silverly pools to raise his nose and sniff the air like a wolf, as if he could actually smell the scent of fear from those he hunted. Well, maybe not Stone. That gritty preacher didn't seem like he frightened easily. But the two teenagers were definitely scared.

He carried the cut-down shotgun in his right hand, down low by his leg, ready to bring it into action in a heartbeat.

I'm coming, he thought. *You worthless fuckers, I'm coming for all your asses.*

He imagined he could hear the sound of Carson and Jenny's hearts pounding frantically in their chests, like panicked drumbeats summoning him to the kill.

He moved further up the trail and paused just short of the teeter-totter. He tilted his head up to look at the giant log jutting overhead, but without anyone to push up on the other end and cause the log to slam down, he knew he wasn't in any danger.

He walked under the log, automatically hustling a little bit as he crossed the point of impact. He might not be in danger, but he still preferred not to spend any more time under the log than necessary.

Just past the teeter-totter, the ground gave way as he stepped on a carefully camouflaged hole. Before he could pull it out, his foot triggered the bear trap at the bottom. The metal teeth snapped shut, shearing through flesh and biting into bone. Blood pulsed onto the ground. Honcho snarled in pain and burned with rage. He was used to being the hunter, not being outfoxed by his prey. He threw back his head and let out an angry, pain-fueled bellow.

"Goddamn you motherfuckers!"

Stone didn't know if Carson or Jenny heard the actual snap of the bear trap closing, but *he* did. But he had no doubt they all heard the angry, profane shout. It sounded like Honcho, and it also sounded like he was less than one hundred yards behind them.

Bet he's moving a lot slower now, Stone thought.

They continued to claw their way through the thickets. They were all exhausted and thorn-scraped and the worse for wear from the various ordeals they had suffered, but Stone couldn't help but feel a sense of grim satisfaction as he heard Honcho's snarls. The bastard deserved every bit of pain tossed his way. If he didn't have the two teenagers to shepherd to safety, Stone would have probably marched back down the trail and dropped Honcho dick-down in the dirt like a rabid dog. Just thinking about all the innocent people the vile piece of garbage had killed made Stone want to put a bullet in his skull. Sure, Stone believed all men could be forgiven by God, but he also believed that some kinds of evil needed to be put down hard. Maybe nobody was beyond redemption, but nobody was beyond justice either.

Stone saw Carson and Jenny looking at him, standing side by side, shoulders lightly touching. The look on Jenny's face was inscrutable, and in a quiet voice she asked, "You think he's dead?"

Another enraged snarl from Honcho ripped through the pre-dawn darkness.

"Not dead," Stone replied. "Just hurting." He tilted his head in the direction of the parking lot. "Come on, let's keep moving. Just a little further and we'll be home free."

The underbrush soon thinned out, and they were able to proceed down the path at a marginally quicker pace.

As they crossed the rickety bridge over the gulch, the black sky started the cyclic process of turning to gray as dawn began to force its will upon the night. By the time they emerged from the woods at the trailhead and walked out into the parking area, the moon still hung full and bloated above them, but the stars had faded, and the heavens were the color of cold ash. Daylight was not far off.

Stone silently thanked God for getting them through the night.

Of course, others had not been so fortunate.

Carson's father, for one.

He glanced at the young man and saw him holding back tears. Carson quickly dabbed at the corner of his eyes. He would no doubt weep uncontrollably when the time came, but seemed to realize now was not that time. Not now, not yet.

Jenny gave him a quick hug and then walked toward the Chevy Blazer, the only vehicle in the parking lot. Stone was relieved to see the organ harvesters had not yet gotten around to making the truck disappear like the other vehicles. Probably had meant to do it today, until Stone's escape had thrown a wrench into their plans. "Nice truck," Jenny said. "Can we run the lights and sirens on the way home?"

"As long as this place is in our rearview mirror," Stone replied, "I don't care what you do."

Jenny tried the passenger door, but it didn't budge. "It's locked."

Stone walked over, flipped the Rossi around in his hands, and used the butt to bust out the window. He reached in through the shattered glass and unlocked the door, then stepped back and grinned at Jenny. "Try again."

She rolled her eyes at him. "Seriously? Carson probably could have picked the lock for you and saved you a broken window. I'm sure he learned that in juvie, along with all those other tricks he was talking about."

Carson shook his head. "The guy who knew how to jimmy locks didn't like me much."

"Why not?"

"Because I broke his damn jaw."

Stone ducked under the steering column and used the pocketknife to pry off the cover. He then yanked out a spaghetti-like mess of wires, found the ones he needed, and started stripping them.

"You broke his jaw?" Jenny was still talking to Carson. "Did you at least have a good reason?"

"Let's just say I prefer to shower alone," Carson replied.

Stone twisted the wires together, and the truck's engine rumbled to life. He sat up and pumped the gas, relishing the roar of the motor as the two teenagers climbed in. "Let's get the hell out of here," he said, hitting the headlights.

Jenny screamed.

Honcho stood in front of the Chevy, bathed in the bright glow of the headlamps that harshly scoured his enraged, pain-twisted features. Blood streamed down his leg from the gruesome wound the bear trap had inflicted, but clearly the bone had not broken, since the bastard was still on his feet.

And he still had the sawed-off shotgun.

Jenny screamed again as Honcho started to raise the weapon, taking an awkward, hobbling step toward the Blazer as he did so.

"Goddamn it." Stone dropped the transmission into Drive and stomped on the gas. As the truck shot forward, he rasped, "Just die, you son of a bitch."

The Chevy rammed into Honcho and folded him over

the hood. The shotgun boomed but only succeeded in blowing off the side mirror.

Stone pinned the pedal to the floor as he drove the Blazer full throttle right through the sign-in station. He heard Honcho howl in pain and anger as the tiny shack practically exploded, wood shards twisting everywhere like shrapnel. The truck powered through the station and slammed into a massive oak, pinning Honcho between the heavy-duty grill guard and the tree trunk. Stone couldn't actually hear it, but he imagined the sickening crunch of the murderer's pelvis being crushed like sledgehammered ice cubes.

Honcho flopped on the hood, unmoving, and the shotgun slipped from his grasp. It skittered across the hood and tumbled off the edge to land on the ground.

"Now is he dead?" Jenny asked.

Stone opened the door, leaned out with the .30-30, and used his last bullet to shoot Honcho in the head. "Yeah, he's dead," he replied.

He dropped the Chevy into Reverse and backed. He breathed a sigh of relief that driving through the sign-in station and smashing the killer against a tree hadn't crippled the truck's mechanics. The grill guard seemed to have done its job and protected the front end. Of course, there were some dents and scratches, but that was it.

Honcho slid off the hood and fell lifelessly to the ground, landing face down in the dirt. The headlights illuminated his wounded leg, the crushed pulp that was his midsection, and the grisly bullet holes in his skull. The slug had drilled him just above his left eye and exited behind his left ear in a mess of shredded brains and bone fragments.

"Man, he sure sucked up a world of hurt," Carson said as he surveyed the gory remains.

"He deserved every bit of it," Jenny replied.

Stone swung the truck around so it faced the road. The tires sprayed gravel all over Honcho's corpse when they drove away. As they headed down the highway, leaving a whole lot of hell behind them, the first rays of the rising sun peeked over the mountains.

Being older—not to mention smaller—than his partners in crime, Rick had not even bothered trying to keep up when Honcho and Goliath headed out to hunt down the escaped prisoners. His stomach churned at the thought of how badly Stone had screwed up their operation just by killing Patch and Doc. When he found Goliath's decimated remains, he knew things had just gotten a whole lot worse.

He picked up the pace, hoping that Honcho would manage to stop the preacher and the two teenagers from getting away. If they could prevent them from getting back to civilization and revealing what Rick and company had been up to back here in the rough country, then there was a chance they could rebuild the operation. Finding another disgraced doctor to properly remove the organs might be difficult, but *difficult* and *impossible* were not the same thing.

He cursed himself for giving in to Goliath and letting him drag Stone out of the cage for some playtime. If not for that miscalculation, the hard-edged preacher would still be rotting in the kennel and none of this crap would have happened. He still couldn't believe Stone had bested the big bastard. Rick knew he had himself to blame just as much as Goliath. He was in charge, the one who called the shots, and in this case, he had called a bad one.

They were in grave danger, no doubt about it.

He heard a single gunshot in the distance.

And somehow, deep down in his guts, he knew *they* were no longer in danger, because there was no more *they*. He sensed that Honcho had just bought the farm and that he, Rick, was now the last member of the gang still standing.

You and me, Stone. We're gonna have ourselves a reckoning.

He'd never killed a preacher before.

But there was a first time for everything.

TWENTY-THREE

BY THE TIME STONE, Carson, and Jenny neared Whisper Falls, the truck was making a strange knocking noise, and steam hissed out from under the battered hood. Apparently, smashing through the sign-in station and ramming into a tree had done more damage than he initially thought. He would have to drop it off at Carcuzzi Automotive in Saranac Lake to get the engine repaired, followed by some bodywork at Wayne Darrah Auto Body. Between the two businesses, they would have the Chevy looking good as new in no time.

But that could wait. He knew eventually they would have to notify the authorities, get checked out at the hospital, answer a million questions—but not yet. On the drive down from Scar Lake, Carson and Jenny had made it clear that before they dealt with investigations and interrogations and evaluations and media attention, they wanted some time to themselves, a few quiet moments to catch their breath and clean up. Food and showers and naps. Stone had agreed to give them some time before he contacted the sheriff's office and kicked things into motion. They were all dirty and exhausted and in desperate need of a respite.

Plus, Stone wanted to get his head right before he confronted Jenny's father.

Stone glanced over Pastor Burke's daughter. Jenny was asleep, slumped against Carson, head leaning on his shoulder. The young man had his arm protectively around her. Their growing affection for one another continued to be obvious.

Stone had tried asking her about how she felt about the horrible things her father had done, but she had remained stubbornly silent. She had asked them to face her father together, but Carson had made it clear that he had no idea how he would react when the time came. Stone hadn't said it out loud, but he felt the same way.

"My father is dead because of him," Carson had said.

"A *lot* of people are dead because of him," Stone added.

Jenny replied, "Maybe my dad *deserves* to die, but it just seems to me like there's been enough death already."

Stone felt sympathy for her. Despite everything she had been through, she was still *Daddy's little girl.* Knowing that her father deserved death, that the two men she now rode with wanted to kill him, couldn't be easy.

But he's a fellow man of the cloth, Stone heard an inner voice say. *Surely you can cut him some slack on that basis alone.*

Stone immediately shut that shit down. Justice didn't take a day off just because the bad guy wore a clerical collar.

The early morning sun cascaded down the pine-covered slopes of the mountains as they rolled into the outskirts of Whisper Falls. A minute later, Stone turned into his driveway and drove up the long stretch of gravel before coming to a stop in front of the three-car garage. He felt bone-weary and was glad he had agreed to give the teenagers some time. He could use a rest himself. He felt dead on his feet.

But at least he wasn't *actually* dead.

Jenny stirred, realizing the truck was no longer moving. She sat up straight and looked at Carson. "Sorry for using your shoulder for a pillow. Hope I didn't drool on you."

His arm was still around her, and he gave her a quick squeeze to let her know it was all right. "Come on," he said, opening the door. "Let's go inside and take a shower."

Jenny arched an eyebrow at him. "Oh, really?"

Carson immediately blushed. "Sorry, I...I didn't mean...we both should take...no, wait...I mean, we both need..." He sighed and gave up. "You know what I meant."

Stone chuckled and shook his head, amused by the boy's awkward discomfort.

Jenny smiled. "Yes, I know what you meant. Just enjoying watching you sweat."

Carson smiled back, clearly relieved, and exited the Chevy. Stone and Jenny climbed out as well. The blood spatter on the hood had dried during the long drive, but it was still there, a dark reminder of the horror they had all survived.

Stone escorted the teenagers inside. Max wandered over to greet them, toenails clicking on the hardwood floor. The Shottie gave Carson a cursory sniff, licked Jenny's hand when she offered it, and then bumped his big, scarred-up head against Stone's thigh to show his affection. He gave Stone a look that seemed to say, *Where ya been, man? It gets real boring when you're not here.*

Stone scratched the dog's ears and then showed Jenny

to one of the spare bedrooms, where he pointed at a dresser. "Don't really have any women's clothes around here, but I'm sure you can scrounge up something in there."

"Something wrong with what I'm wearing?" Jenny asked with a smirk.

Stone looked at her filthy rags and said, "Nothing that some gasoline and a match won't cure."

He showed her the bathroom and where to find the towels, shampoo, and soap. "It's all yours," he said. "I'll get Carson set up in the other guest room, and he can use the shower when you're done. I'll be in my bedroom, cleaning up."

He closed the door behind him as he left.

Jenny spent a full thirty minutes in the shower. She half-expected Carson to make a play and try to join her, and she found herself unsure whether she would reject such a brazen advance or not. But apparently, he was a gentleman, because he left her alone. As the hot water rinsed away the grime and revealed her thin, bony, scarred, abused body, she was thankful to be showering solo. She might have been pretty once, but not anymore.

She washed her hair four times and used a whole bar of soap to scrub herself from scalp to soles, scouring her skin until it glowed pink. It still felt surreal that she had been rescued. How many times had she prayed? How many times had she vented her hopes—and hopelessness—to Mr. Joe, her eight-legged confidant? And now here she was, safe and sound, albeit a bit worse for wear. Honcho, Doc, Patch, and Goliath might not have raped or killed her, but they had been cruel captors nonetheless. The scars on her body proved that.

She wondered what Carson would think if he saw her naked, all her wounds and secrets laid bare. She tried not to imagine what it would be like to have him here in the shower with her, the hot water streaming over his hard muscles.

What in the world is wrong with me? she wondered. *You'd think after everything I've been through, romance would be the last thing on my mind. Besides, he wants to kill my father.*

She abruptly reached out and turned the shower faucet all the way to *Cold*. She stood under the freezing spray until she was shivering and the fires of attraction had been, if not fully extinguished, at least doused into smoldering embers.

She climbed out of the shower and then rummaged through the dresser and closet in the bedroom. Obviously, there was no women's underwear—would have been weird to find out Pastor Stone was a crossdresser—but she found a pair of boxers that worked well enough. After years of dressing in dirty rags, it felt good to wear clean, comfortable cotton.

She found a toothbrush still sealed in its original package tucked into the back corner of the medicine cabinet behind a bottle of Excedrin. As she brushed her teeth, she thought about Mike Donner, Carson's dad, and how he was dead because of what her own father had done. She tried to force herself to see things from Carson's perspective, the grief and anger and hunger for vengeance he must be feeling.

The bristles of the toothbrush made her gums bleed, and when she spat into the sink, the white paste was funneled with red. She managed to get the top off the mouthwash bottle and swished some around in her mouth. The antiseptic burned and made her eyes water, but it was a good, cleansing burn.

She found a hairbrush in a drawer and started working the snarls out of her unkempt mane. She'd gotten some of them out in the shower, using half a bottle of conditioner in the process, but she needed a brush to finish the job. Took nearly ten minutes and more than a few winces at some of the nastier clumps, but she got it done, her still-damp hair falling smooth and tangle-free down to her shoulders.

Back in the bedroom, she found a simple white t-shirt and a pair of men's jeans that she cinched around her waist with a belt and then rolled up the cuffs. She stood in front of the mirror and decided she didn't look half bad, given everything she'd been through.

And thinking about all she had been through made her think about her father again. "Damn it, Dad, what were you thinking?" she said softly, trembling at her image in the mirror, staring at herself, at her scarred, abused body. He had allowed it to happen. She struggled against the rage and self-pity that she felt rising up to consume her.

She lost.

"Fuck you!" The words just burst out of her, like an emotional dam breaking. "Fuck you! Fuck you! Fuck you!" She wasn't even sure who she was raging against. She slumped against the wall and wept. Not because she wanted to, but because she couldn't help it. She needed a release, and something deep down inside that she couldn't control was going to make sure she got it, whether she liked it or not.

She pushed away from the wall and stumbled out of the bathroom, back into the bedroom, where she fell face down on the bed and cried into a pillow that smelled slightly musty from lack of use.

She heard footsteps outside the door, followed by Stone and Carson's lowered voices discussing who should check on her. She heard Carson say, "I've got it," and a moment later, he gently knocked and entered the room.

He sat down on the edge of the bed. "What's wrong?"

Jenny kept her face pressed into the pillow, so her words were muffled when she answered, "Nothing. Everything."

"That doesn't exactly clear things up."

Still not looking at him, she said, "Why did this happen? Damn them. Damn them all straight to hell."

Carson put a hand on the small of her back. He meant it to be comforting, but Jenny couldn't ignore the tantalizing feelings his touch generated within her. She found herself wishing his hand would slide lower, do things other than simply comfort. Then she mentally shook her head and thought, *No way would he want me. Not after everything they did to me. Not with all these scars on my body.*

Aloud, she said, "Don't touch me. I'm ugly."

He kept his hand on her back. "You're not ugly," he said. "Don't say that."

She lifted her head and turned over to look at him. "How can you say that? They cut the shit out of me whenever they were bored. I've got more scars than Christ after He got scourged."

Carson hesitated, seemingly unsure of what to say, how to respond. No surprise, really, Jenny thought. He'd been locked up at a pretty young age and didn't have much experience with talking to girls, let alone one like her who had suffered trauma and tragedy. Besides, he had his own crap to deal with, now that both his parents were dead. Her father might have done some terrible things, but at least he was still alive.

For now, anyway.

"You don't have to say anything," Jenny said. "Not your job to make me feel better."

Carson's face turned red. "Sorry, I just...just don't have much experience with girls."

She smiled. "Thanks for trying to help. By the way, you're cute when you blush."

Unbeknownst to her, Carson was thinking that he really liked to see her smile. The lines of hardship etched in her face faded to almost nothing when she smiled, defining her natural prettiness with extra depth. Free and freshly cleaned, her true grace and beauty shone through. Carson struggled to keep his eyes off her and found that he didn't really want to.

But while Jenny might not have known exactly what he was thinking, she was definitely aware of his intense stare. She awkwardly averted her eyes and then looked at him again, feeling her own face turn red.

He gave her a roguish grin. "By the way, you're cute when you blush."

"You're such a jerk." But she smiled when she said it and then asked, "Now what?"

"Now I guess we find something to eat, and then..." His voice trailed off, and his grin faded as he looked away from her, unwilling to meet her eyes as he finished his thought. "And then we go pay your dad a visit."

A long silence followed. When Carson dared to meet her gaze again, Jenny stared at him intently. "Carson," she said, "I need to ask you something."

"Okay."

She took a deep breath, almost said what she was really thinking, and then changed her mind and asked, "Do you think Stone has any frozen pizza?"

Carson blinked at her. "Really? Pizza? That's what you want to talk about?"

"I don't want to talk about my father."

At their request, Stone fixed them a DiGiorno's pepperoni pizza, complemented by a bag of Cool Ranch Doritos and washed down with Mountain Dew. Sensing they needed some time alone, he grabbed a slice for himself and headed outside with Max to check on Rocky. The two teenagers took the food into the bedroom, turned on the TV, and watched a *Bonanza* rerun as they ate.

"I used to hate Mountain Dew," Jenny said. "But right now, it tastes like the best thing I ever drank." She picked up another piece of pizza and started chowing down. It was her third slice. Skinny as she was, Carson figured he should probably let her eat the whole thing.

"My dad always had Diet Dew around the house," Carson said. "Not sure why, since it's not like he needed to worry about his weight." He swallowed the sudden lump in his throat at the thought of his father. Stone had promised they would go back for the remains so he could give his dad a proper burial next to his mother. He put down his slice of pizza, no longer hungry. "Besides, he was pretty much a drunk after my mom died, so he never drank soda. Nothing but vodka, whiskey, rum, tequila, and something called Rumple Minze."

"What's Rumple Minze?" Jenny asked.

"One hundred proof peppermint schnapps."

"Sounds disgusting."

"It's a touch nastier than drinking Bud Light, that's for sure."

"I'd always heard Bud Light is for sissies who can't handle real beer."

"Did you just call me a sissy?"

"Just telling you what I've heard."

She took a swig of Mountain Dew, and it apparently went down the wrong tube, because she started coughing. Carson patted her on the back and chuckled. "Amateur."

She leaned over until the coughing spell passed. When she sat back up and turned to him, their faces were kissing close.

So that's what they did.

The kiss was light, hesitant, unsure. Carson felt Jenny freeze up for a second, but when he tried to pull back, she moved into him, kissing harder. He pulled her close, hand tracing the curve of her spine. He stopped kissing her long enough to softly ask, "Are you sure you want to do this?"

"Shut up and kiss me," she said.

Carson felt heat pouring through them. Not really love or even lust, but just a desperate drive to affirm life in the aftermath of death. It was something they both needed.

No more talking. He kissed her with everything he had, sensing she wanted, *needed*, the same thing he did—a few moments of feeling alive, a few moments to ease the pain in their hearts and souls, a few heartbeats of heaven to make them momentarily forget their hells.

Rick drove back to his sporting goods store in Saranac Lake after spending all morning burying his partners deep in the woods, in a desolate place where he knew no one would ever find them unless they brought in cadaver dogs and knew exactly where to look. He hadn't bothered saying any words over their unmarked graves. He didn't much give care if they went to heaven or hell. God would deal with them as He saw fit, and nothing Rick could say or pray would change that.

He almost hightailed it up to Canada once Stone and the two teenagers got away, but decided he was too old for a life on the run. Besides, he ached for another confrontation with Stone and decided he would rather go out in a blaze of glory than hunker down like a scared rabbit, waiting for the law to catch up with him. No, sometimes a man just had to face his problems head-on and to hell with the consequences. Look the devil dead in the eye, kick him in his bright red cock, and reap whatever consequences you had coming.

He was covered head to toe in dirt and tired right down to the bone. But he couldn't rest. Not yet. He still had miles to go, as the saying went.

He tried not to think about everything he had lost today, the profitable operation that had come tumbling down. They should have just left Michael Donner and his delinquent son alone. Actually, he should have just killed the coward the same night he put a bullet in his wife's head. Then he could have cleaned things up by executing Carson, too. If the whole family had been sucking maggots, none of this would have happened.

But you could bet your ass he was going to put the last member of the Donner family six feet under. And he would do it with the same gun he used to kill the boy's mother. He would drive out to Whisper Falls, kill that worthless, meddling preacher and that bitch Jenny, and then shoot Carson Donner right in the face with the same gun he used to blow his mom's brains out. He would do it for the dead, for Doc and Patch and Goliath and Honcho. And hell yeah, he would do it for himself, for his own damn satisfaction.

Time to kill.

He used his thumbprint to unlock a small biometric gun safe, pulled out a Colt .45 with a dragon etched into the walnut handle, and threaded a suppressor onto the barrel. He referred to the pistol as his *thrill kill* gun, the weapon he used when he invaded homes and killed not for business, but for pure sport. Slaughtering wayward hikers and lost hunters deep in the Scar Lake backwoods was nothing more than a profit-generating enterprise, but forcing his way into a home in the middle of town and playing his sick, twisted game was pure pleasure.

Unfortunately, in an area as small as the tri-lakes region, he had to be careful not to indulge too frequently. He carved a notch into the handle of the Colt every time he thrill-killed, and there were only six notches. Lisa Donner was represented by the sixth and final notch. Well, final for now. He would add a seventh notch after he put a bullet in her son.

He grabbed a box of .45 ACP ammo and headed out to finish the hunt.

Swept up in their emotions, Carson and Jenny lost track of time. They didn't even hear Stone come back in the house until he stood in the doorway and cleared his throat. Then they both jumped and hurriedly moved away from each other like a couple of middle schoolers caught in a necking session.

"Having fun?" Stone grinned. The morning sun speared through the partially open shades.

"Sorry." Carson looked sheepish. "Guess we, uh, got caught up in the moment."

"All good," Stone said.

Jenny looked at him. "Time to go?"

"Needs to happen at some point."

"Yeah, I guess you're right."

"You don't want to see your father?"

"Yes and no."

Stone nodded. "I get that."

Carson stood up. Stone felt a subtle shift—their blissful moments of passion now ended, replaced by grim tension. "I want to see your father," he said. "I really enjoyed that kiss, but it doesn't change how I feel. Your father sent my father—and me, for that matter—to be killed. I want him dead."

"I know," Jenny said quietly. "I won't lie—I hoped whatever you feel for me, and what I feel for you, would make you think twice about getting revenge against my father, but that's not why I kissed you. I think that was just something we both needed after everything we've been through. But if it had made you change your mind about what you want to do to my dad, well, that would have been a nice bonus."

Carson didn't say anything for several long moments. He just stood there and looked at her, eyes hooded and thoughtful. Finally, he said, "Let's just see how it goes."

Stone left the room, saying, "I'll wait for you guys in the truck."

Outside, he stood by the driver's side door and looked through the broken window at the Rossie .30-30 lever-action lying in the cab. He had also retrieved his Colt Cobra .38 snub-nosed revolver, now riding in a leather holster on his belt. He thought about what he wanted to do to Pastor Perry Burke and wondered what he would do if Jenny tried to stop him.

TWENTY-FOUR

PASTOR BURKE SAT behind his desk as the sun came up, trying to squeeze in some early morning Bible reading. Sometimes, sitting in his empty house drinking coffee in silence was just too depressing, so he came to the church instead. He knew God was everywhere, not just in church, but he always felt closer to Him here. It also seemed easier to confess his sins in this hallowed building instead of at his kitchen table.

And God knew he had a lot of sins to confess.

His well-worn study Bible was spread before him, cracked open to the Book of Luke, chapter fifteen the story of the prodigal son, his all-time favorite scripture passage. He had a daughter, not a son, but he still knew what it felt like to desperately wish your child was safe at home with you.

He nearly jumped out of his skin as his office door smashed open. The knob banged into the wall with enough force to punch a hole in the sheetrock.

Stone stormed into the room with a rifle in his hand and anger in his eyes. Burke knew at that exact moment that he was a dead man. Stone appeared cold and merciless, the ice in his gaze anything but forgiving. And frankly, Burke knew he didn't deserve any forgiveness. He had done terrible things, and there was blood all over his hands.

Stone marched across the office and shoved the muzzle of the .30-30 right between the pastor's eyes, pressing hard enough to nearly split the skin. "Hey, brother," he said. "Bet you're surprised to see me."

Burke kept absolutely still. Sudden moves were ill-advised with a rifle against his forehead. Maybe he deserved to die, but he wasn't in a hurry to make it happen. The only thing he moved were his lips. "Stone," he said, managing to keep his voice much calmer than he actually felt, "I must admit that this visit is unexpected, but are you sure shoving a gun in a man of God's face is the best way to proceed?"

"Man of God?" Stone sneered at the words. "You've got some balls calling yourself that. You set them up. You sent them out there to be slaughtered, and now Mike Donner is dead. Not to mention God knows how many other people. All dead, all because of you. So, what you need to do right now is give me one good reason not to pull this trigger."

Burke felt like he was going to wet his pants. Never had he been as hyper-aware of his own fragile mortality as he was right now. He searched for words that might spare him. "You don't understand," he said, desperation in his voice. "I didn't have a choice. Those psychos have my daughter."

"Had."

"What?"

"They *had* your daughter," Stone corrected. "Past tense."

"What are you talking about?"

At that moment, Jenny walked into the office. "Hi, Dad."

"Oh my God! Jenny!" Burke started to rise.

Stone pushed him back down with the rifle. "I don't think so. Keep your ass glued to the chair."

Burke complied, and once Stone was satisfied that he wouldn't try to get back up, he moved aside and let Jenny approach her father. She walked around the desk, tears in her eyes, and then abruptly threw herself into his arms. For a few moments, she was nothing more than a frightened little girl, and he was nothing more than her comforting daddy. For a few precious heartbeats, their reunion was joyous, sins forgotten, no barriers between them. They wept together as Stone stood by and watched.

But of course, the moment could not last forever. Jenny finally stepped back and used the back of her hand to wipe away the tear-tracks that silvered her face.

Burke looked at his daughter with haunted eyes, taking in the scars that laced her gaunt frame. "Oh, honey, what did they do to you?" Seeing her like this broke his heart. *Not* seeing her for all these years had almost been easier than having her standing before him now. During her captivity, he had at least been able to imagine that she wasn't being harmed. But now he was forced to face the stark proof that such naïve imaginings had been grossly untrue. Jenny's every scar was a stinging condemnation that lanced him deeply.

Jenny stared at him and it was plain to see that she was no longer a scared little daddy's girl who needed hugs and solace. That moment had passed. Now she was a survivor. An angry survivor who demanded answers. "Trust me, Dad," she said, "you don't want to know what they did to me. But what about you? What did *you* do?"

Burke just looked at her. He had nothing to say. There was nothing he *could* say.

"Exactly," Jenny said. "Nothing. That's exactly what you did. Absolutely nothing."

Burke thought about reaching out to her, but decided that would probably be a mistake. Stone still looked like he was just begging for a reason to put a bullet in him. Instead, he sat still and tried to offer justification for what he had done. "I did what they asked," he said. "I sent them people so they wouldn't kill you. They kept their word, right? Honey, I know they did some terrible things to you, but at least you're alive…" His voice trailed off as he realized he wasn't getting through to her.

Jenny looked like she wanted to slap him. "And how many people died to keep me that way?" she demanded. "How many people did you send to be slaughtered by those sons of bitches so I could stay alive?"

Burke bowed his head, tears dripping onto his shoes. "I didn't have a choice, sweetheart."

"Of course you had a choice," she said. "You could have tried to save me. You're my father, and you did nothing. Nothing! Except send innocent people to be butchered."

Her accusing stare cut him like a scalpel, as if she wanted to peel back his flesh and peer into his soul to see if there was anything in there worth salvaging. Love glowed in one of her eyes while loathing burned in the other, and plainly etched on her face was a war between the two emotional extremes.

Burke had no response, no words that could make it right. What he had done was unforgivable. He knew that. But that didn't stop him from saying, "I'm so sorry, Jenny. But please—*please,* sweetheart—can you ever forgive me?"

"I don't know, Dad. Part of me wants to, but the

other part of me can't forget that you left me in a cage to rot and be tortured by those creeps." She stared at him, hard and cold, for several long moments before her face abruptly softened. "All I can promise you is this—I'll try. I'll try to forgive you, but it's going to take time."

Stone broke his menacing silence. "And you might not have a whole lot of that left."

Burke licked his lips nervously. "Listen, Stone, I—"

"Save it!" Stone rasped. "Nothing you can say will make things right. Nothing will change the fact that because of you, people are dead. If there were words that could turn back time, maybe I would let you talk. But there's not, so do us both a favor and shut your mouth."

Jenny glanced at Stone and then looked back at her father with sadness on her face. She leaned down and kissed him on the cheek. "Bye, Daddy," she said softly, then turned and walked away.

Burke's heart constricted as she headed toward the office door, leaving him to his fate. That same heart began hammering wildly as he realized this might be the last time he ever saw her, that just minutes from now, maybe even seconds, he might very well be dead. There was no mercy in Stone's cold eyes and no chance on God's green earth of surviving a point-blank rifle blast. At this range, Stone couldn't miss if he wanted to.

Jenny stopped next to Stone, put her hand on his arm, and said, "I'm not going to ask you to forgive him—I can't ask you to do something I'm not sure I can do myself—but I am going to ask you not to pull that trigger." Her voice thickened with emotion, and she swallowed hard. "He's my father. The only one I have. Killing him won't bring Carson's dad back. It will just leave me without one, too." Her hand slipped away from his arm. "We'll be waiting for you outside."

When she was gone, Stone looked at Burke, feeling the anger, the deep-rooted code of primal justice, smoldering inside him like hot coals. He wondered what the other pastor was feeling. His daughter had been abducted, and having lost a daughter himself, Stone could at least relate to that sense of pain and loss. But that didn't absolve the man of blame.

Stone felt the warrior within demanding blood, retribution, a reckoning for all the brutality and butchery Burke had played a part in. As always, it was not easily denied, doing its damnedest to overpower his preacher side, the part that believed in grace and mercy and second chances.

Fear-sweat oozed down Burke's face and left an oily sheen on his upper lip as he waited for the gunshot that would send him to his eternal judgment.

Stone stared at him, teeth clenched, eyes colder than a dead viper. He raised the rifle, finger tight against the trigger. But he didn't squeeze it. Not yet.

What are you waiting for?

Burke suddenly broke down into sob, clasping his hands in front of him in the classic prayer formation as he desperately pleaded with the man who seemed on the verge of killing him. "Please, Stone! I don't want to die!"

Stone stepped forward and tucked the barrel of the Rossi .30-30 under Burke's chin. He levered the disgraced pastor's head up and back. If he fired now, the bullet would blow out the top of Burke's skull and paint the picture of Jesus on the wall behind him with hot, wet gore. His lips peeled back from his teeth as he snarled, "Too bad."

"NO, WAIT!"

Stone pulled the trigger.

Burke screamed.

Click!

The firing pin fell on an empty chamber.

Burke shit himself.

His muscles suddenly failed him, and he fell from his chair to sprawl on the carpet as the stench of his shame filled the small office.

Stone towered above him, the unloaded .30-30 canted over his shoulder. "I'll let God deal with you," he rasped. "Until then, you live with it."

Burke curled into a sobbing mess. Stone still felt like stomping the guy's head into a broken eggshell, but he had already made the decision to let Burke live, not for his own sake, but for Jenny's.

As he walked through the foyer toward the front door, he fed cartridges into the rifle. Rick was still out there somewhere, and until he was caught or killed, Stone planned to always have a loaded weapon within reach. Hell, he always did anyway. He'd sooner forget his pants than his pistol.

He had his head down as he pushed open the front door of the church to walk outside, but it snapped up when he heard Jenny's strangled cry—what he saw sent fear slamming through him.

Rick stood by the truck, holding Jenny hostage in front of him. One arm snaked around her throat like a python, while the other hand pressed a gun to her temple. Carson was down on the ground nearby, sitting up but looking groggy, holding a hand to the back of his head where Stone assumed Rick had thumped him with the butt of his pistol.

Stone's eyes narrowed as he recognized the pistol stuck against Jenny's head. A Colt .45 with a dragon etched on the notched grips. The same weapon Griz had mentioned when telling him the cold case story about the unsolved murder of Lisa Donner.

"Where'd you get that gun?" he asked Rick.

Rick's face was caked with dirt, so his teeth gleamed shockingly white when he grinned and said, "I've had this piece of hot lead hardware a long time."

Carson pulled his hand away from his head. Blood stained his fingers. Looked like the pistol-whipping had split open his scalp. "So, you're the one who killed my mother." It wasn't a question, and Carson gritted the revelation through clenched teeth.

"Depends on how ya look at it," Rick said. "Way I see it, your father killed your mother by being a coward, but I guess if you wanna get all technical about it, then yeah, I put a bullet through your momma's brain."

"I'm gonna fucking kill you."

"Yeah, yeah, yeah," Rick drawled. "Spare me the threats and tough guy talk. I think we all know how this plays out, right?"

Stone looked at Jenny. Her face was a mask of fear, and her thin body trembled in Rick's grasp. But with that pistol pressed against her head, there wasn't much he could do but wait it out, see how things progressed, and pray for an opening. Still, that didn't stop him from growling, "Let her go."

"We'll see about that," Rick replied. "Kind of depends on Carson over there." He waggled the gun without moving the muzzle away from Jenny's head. "See those notches in the handle, boy? Pretty cool, huh? That sixth one is your mother, by the way."

"You're a real piece of shit, you know that?" Stone said. "I'm gonna send you to hell and smile when I do it."

"Now, that's not a very nice thing for a preacher to say," Rick replied. "Might wanna study up on yer job description. You're s'pposed to save souls from hell, not send 'em there."

"In your case, I'll make an exception."

"Not before I put another notch on this gun." Rick looked over at Carson. "But whether that notch is for you or this bitch is entirely in your hands."

Stone felt his blood run cold. The rifle felt like a useless, leaden weight in his hands. With Rick holding Jenny in front of him and a gun to her head, there was no way for Stone to get off a kill shot. He was fast, but not fast enough to raise the rifle and put a slug in Rick's eyeball before the son of a bitch splattered her skull with a point-blank .45 bullet.

Jenny whimpered in terror. Her eyes sought Stone, desperately pleading.

Stone felt a cold, hard knot coil deep in his guts. He hated the helpless feeling he had right now. Through gritted teeth, he said, "Rick, we'll figure this out. Don't kill her."

"Don't kill her?" Rick's voice dripped with amused malice. "That's entirely up to our boy Carson. You see, I'm gonna give him a chance to save this little dolly. Same chance I gave his worthless father all those years ago."

Carson seemed to know exactly what he was supposed to say, the script he was expected to follow. "I'll do anything you want. Just don't hurt her."

"Glad to hear it." Rick glanced at Stone. "Lose the rifle."

"And if I don't?"

Rick screwed the muzzle of the .45 even tighter against Jenny's temple. "You know the answer to that."

Stone hesitated, but realized he didn't really have a choice. He did as instructed, dropping the Rossi on the ground.

"Now take that pistol off your hip and toss it over to the lad," Rick ordered.

Stone shucked the Colt Cobra out of its holster and threw it so it landed at Carson's feet.

"Pick it up," Rick commanded, "and tuck the barrel under yer chin nice an' tight. Right there above the lump in yer throat."

While Stone desperately tried to figure a way out of this mess that didn't end with one or both of the teenagers dead, Carson slowly obeyed Rick's instructions. As the muzzle of the revolver touched the skin under his jaw, right next to a frantically pulsing vein, the desperate horror churning through him was visible for anyone to see. Sweat exploded from every pore.

Now he knows what his father felt like, Stone thought.

"Good boy," said Rick. "Now, I think ya know what I want ya to do next."

Stone interjected. "Why don't you stop hiding behind a helpless girl? Let her go, and we can settle this like men."

Rick grinned. "Nice try, preacher man."

"What's the matter, ain't got the balls?"

Rick's grin abruptly vanished. "I'll bury my balls in this bitch's ass if her boyfriend doesn't pull that goddamned trigger."

Stone looked at Carson. "Don't do it."

"I watched my mother die," Carson said. "I can't let the same thing happen to Jenny."

"Do it!" Rick snapped. "Or so help me God, I'll blow the little whore's brains out."

Stone knew Rick wasn't bluffing. Carson knew it, too. The young man placed his finger in the pistol's trigger guard. A few pounds of pressure and it would all be over. He would join his mother and father in whatever waited beyond the business end of a bullet. He wouldn't even feel the slug burn through his head.

"Carson," Stone said. "Look at me."

Carson hesitated, seemingly trying to buy some time. He looked at Stone, as if begging him to find a resolution that didn't require him to kill himself.

Jenny stared at him intensely. She couldn't move her head with the .45 pressed against it, but her eyes conveyed a message. *No. Don't do it.*

"Ain't got the guts, hey?" Rick taunted. "Your pussy of a father had the same problem. So, I'll give you the same incentive I gave him. I'm gonna rattle off a five-count. If I reach five an' you ain't put a bullet through her head, then I'm gonna put one through this bitch's. Got it? Right here—"

"Yeah, I know the rest." Carson cut him off. "Right here, right now, I am God. Life or death, the choice is mine. I've heard this shit before, remember?"

"Ya gotta admit, I know how to make a lasting impression," Rick said. Then, without warning, he started the countdown. "One."

Stone felt any fragile shreds of hope unraveling fast. Carson was a dead man. He steeled himself to make some kind of desperation play that he already knew would fail. Once Rick got to four, he would have to do something to try and save Jenny…and probably get her killed in the process.

God, we need a miracle right about now.

"Two."

Suddenly, the doors of the church flew open, and Perry Burke raced down the steps screaming, "Get your hands off my daughter!" His hair was wild, and his pants reeked of excrement as he charged Rick with the recklessness of a man who has nothing left to lose.

Rick swung the .45 away from Jenny's head long enough to put a bullet in Burke.

Jenny screamed, *"NO!"* as her father spun around like a blood-spraying dervish before tumbling awkwardly to the ground.

It was all the opening Stone needed. He flipped the .30-30 into the air with his boot, grabbed it with snake-strike speed, and without hesitation fired a round right into Rick's surprised face. The hollow-point cored through his right eye and blew open the back of his head. Somehow, he stayed on his feet, staggering backward, his body not yet receiving the message that he was dead. The dragon-etched .45 fell from his twitching fingers to land in the dirt.

Carson took the Colt Cobra out from under his chin and fired his own bullet at the man responsible for the death of his mother and father. It caught Rick in the throat. Carson fired again, and Rick's remaining eye disappeared as the bullet vaporized the socket.

This time, Rick went down and stayed there.

Carson approached the body. He leveled the gun at the shuddering corpse and emptied the pistol into Rick's unfeeling flesh, the shots booming through the mountain air. The dead man jerked from the close-range impacts of the slugs ripping into him, blood spouting from the wounds.

"When you get to hell," Carson snarled, "tell the devil that the last thing you ate was my fucking bullet."

Nearby, Pastor Burke struggled to get on his feet. Blood soaked his side where Rick's bullet had struck him. He made it upright, but his legs immediately buckled. He reached out for support. Stone caught one arm, and Jenny took the other, bearing his weight.

"It's all right, Dad," she said. "We've got you."

Burke's face was pale, but he managed to smile

weakly at his daughter. Blood from his wound—upon closer inspection, Stone gauged the bullet had bounced off a rib—dripped onto the ground.

Jenny looked at Stone. "We need to get him to the hospital."

Stone nodded. "Help me get him in the truck."

With Carson's help, they managed to load Burke into the Chevy Blazer, stretched out in the cargo hold on some emergency blankets. The stench from his soiled pants caused the air to reek, and blood leaked everywhere, but nobody cared. Burke's reckless, sacrificial charge at Rick had been the catalyst that saved the day. He had earned the right to bleed all over the place.

In the cab, Jenny sat in the middle, slumped against Carson. "I don't want to lose him," she said. "I know he did a lot of bad things, but he did it all to save me, and he saved me again today."

"He's a father," Stone said, thinking about his own daughter that he had lost. "And a father will always be there when you need him."

"You've got me, too," Carson said.

She pulled his face down and kissed him softly. "Thank you."

Stone drove away as the morning sun bathed the church steeple in golden light.

TWENTY-FIVE

HOURS LATER, surrounded by luxury, Stone stared with distaste at the man sitting across from him. He had paid Mason Xavier a visit to let him know his brother-in-law was dead, along with the mercenary he had hired, but that his nephew had been brought back alive.

"So I heard," Xavier said. They sat at a glass patio table beside an Olympic-size in-ground swimming pool, the smell of chlorine heavy in the air, sunrays sparking diamonds off the water. Xavier held a glass of wine in his hand. Stone had declined a drink. "I also heard that you solved the mystery of my sister's murder, as well as rescued the Burke girl that everyone thought was dead. Looks like you're a hero yet again, Sheriff."

"I'm no hero. Just a man who does what needs to be done."

"I also heard that everyone involved is now dead."

"Pretty much."

Xavier nodded in satisfaction. "Never doubted I had the right man for the job."

"Didn't do it for you. Think I made that pretty clear."

"I don't care who you killed them for, as long as you killed them," Xavier said.

"They died because they had it coming."

Xavier tilted his head as if studying a specimen in a museum. "Why can't you just admit what you are, Stone?"

"What would that be?"

"A killer."

"I only kill when it needs to be done."

Xavier snorted. "You and I both know that's not true."

"You don't know shit, Mason. I'm not some thrill-kill cowboy who gets his rocks off by making people bite the dust." Stone wasn't sure why he was bothering to defend himself to a crime boss, but he forged ahead anyway. "Sometimes justice demands blood."

"Some might call that kind of thinking barbaric, a left-over relic from less civilized times."

"And I would call those people fools," Stone replied.

Xavier leaned back in his chair and swirled the wine in his glass with idle elegance, his eyes fixed on Stone's face. "You know what I think, Sheriff? I think you like it. I think all the killing gets your blood hot. Makes you feel like some kind of avenging angel, am I right? Like you're indulging in the savage side of righteousness."

Stone's jaw tightened. "You think I enjoy dropping bodies? That the level of hate you think I have in me?"

"I don't think it's hate. I simply think you like playing God, deciding who deserves your particular brand of justice, who lives, who dies."

"What do you know about justice? You traffic in blood and try to hide it all under the disguise of a businessman. When I spill blood, it's all about setting the wrong things right."

Xavier smiled arrogantly. "You talk about disguises.

Believe me, sheriff, justice is just a pretty word people use to make revenge sound noble."

"You're wrong," Stone said. "Sometimes justice and revenge look similar, but they're different animals."

"They may be different animals," Xavier replied, "but they're the same species."

"You're entitled to your opinion. Good thing I don't answer to you."

"Of course," Xavier drawled sarcastically, "you answer to *God,* right?"

"Basically, yeah."

Xavier made a scoffing noise. "The same God that let my sister's killer walk free for all these years? The same God who let Mike die, who turned my nephew into an orphan? The same God who let that poor girl rot in a cage? I've seen your God, Stone, and I am not impressed."

"Given your track record, I'm betting He feels the same way about you."

"But He loves *you,* right?" Xavier waved a hand in Stone's direction. "You go out there and play judge, jury, and executioner. To hell with the courts. To hell with the system. Justice is in your hands, and you think God is okay with that?"

"You're putting a lot of words in my mouth that I never said."

"What you do, Stone, isn't justice. It's punishment. And it doesn't become righteous just because you say it is."

Stone stood up, chair legs scraping against the flagstone decking. He'd had enough of this crap. He had already wasted too much time arguing with a man who probably deserved a bullet as much as anyone Stone had ever killed. "Think what you want, Mason. I don't owe you any explanation for how I operate or how I answer to

God Almighty. When He judges me someday, I'll pay attention. When you judge me, it doesn't mean a damn thing. You're just a dirtbag hiding in a fancy suit, pretending to be noble."

Xavier replied, "You're no better than me, Stone. You just wear your sins differently. Mine are cloaked in tailored suits. Yours are hidden behind a badge and a Bible."

Stone stepped toward the exit. "We all answer for our sins someday, Mason. You might want to remember that."

"That a threat?"

"Make of it what you will."

Xavier's eyes narrowed. "If I'm as dangerous as you say I am, then you would be wise to think twice about crossing me."

Stone rasped, "Fuck off, Mason."

And walked out the door.

Stone's next visit was to Holly, and that scared him more than anything he had faced up in Scar Lake.

She let him in, which he took as a good sign—he hadn't been sure she would even open the door—and listened quietly as they sat on the couch, and he told her everything that had happened the last few days.

"You've got a knack for getting into some real scrapes," she said when he had finished telling the story.

"Comes with the job."

"You and I both know it's more than that," Holly replied. "For whatever reason, you're drawn to trouble. Like a moth to a flame, as the saying goes. You can't just sit on your hands and do nothing when wicked people are doing wicked things. It's the cowboy in you."

The cowboy or the warrior, Stone thought. *Call it what you will.*

He said, "I came to Whisper Falls to put all the violence behind me."

"Guess God had different plans for you."

"You really think God prefers me with a gun in my hand instead of a Bible?"

"You've got two hands." Holly shrugged. "You're the expert on God, not me, but from where I'm standing, it kind of looks like maybe He wants you to do both."

"Or maybe that's just what I tell myself to justify what I do."

"You'll figure it out." Holly reached over and lightly touched his shoulder. Her hand felt warm. "No matter what, I'm glad you're still alive."

"You sure about that?"

"Don't go all dramatic on me, Luke. Asking you to figure out where things stand with your ex-wife isn't the same thing as wanting you dead."

"Just checking."

She gave him a soft smile. "Listen, I know you love me, and I love you. I just think you have some unresolved emotions, deep down, about Theresa. I mean, she's clearly got some for you."

"She was drunk, that's all."

"And when she was drunk, she wanted her past back. She wanted *you* back."

"I can't help it that I have a past, Holly. We all have pasts. But what I *can* tell you is that Theresa can't have me back because I'm in love with you and only you. So, tell me what I need to do, because I don't want to lose you."

She reached over and took his hand. "You're not losing me, cowboy. But I'm not sharing you with another woman, with the ghost of a past, broken relationship."

"That sounds an awful lot like a breakup."

"We're not breaking up, Luke. Just slowing things down."

"I'm not sure what that means, Holly."

"It means no next step," she replied. "It means we're together, but we're not *all the way* together. Not yet."

"So, you're saying we've still got some shit to figure out, but you still love me?"

She moved closer. "Something like that. Now shut up and kiss me, cowboy."

He obliged.

The next morning, Stone called Deputy Valentine into his office.

The deputy pulled the door closed behind him and stood in front of Stone's desk like a soldier reporting for duty at boot camp. "You wanted to see me?"

"Relax, Cade. Have a seat. I didn't bring you in here for a butt-chewing."

Valentine allowed some of the rigidness to ease from his frame as he sat down in one of the chairs in front of the desk and let out a sigh. "No, I figured you called me in here to gloat."

"I come across as a gloater to you?"

Valentine shrugged. "Not really, but I wouldn't blame you if you did. I walk in here a few days ago, tell you I'm gunning for your badge. So, what do you do? Go out and take down a black-market organ harvesting operation, rescue a missing girl, and solve the Donner cold case, all in one fell swoop." He shook his head as if he couldn't believe it. "I have to admit, sheriff, it's pretty impressive, and I wouldn't hold it against you one bit if you wanted to rub it in my face a little bit. The whole town is calling you a hero. Don't worry, I'm not going to run against you in the next election. Not now. I wouldn't have a snowball's chance in hell of winning against you."

"That may be true," Stone said. "But what if you didn't have to run against me?"

Valentine looked puzzled. "What are you talking about?"

"I'm thinking about stepping down," Stone said. "Focus more on being a preacher. I'm guessing if I threw my support behind you, the county would make you the next sheriff."

"You're...*resigning?*"

"Thinking about it." Stone paused. "Kind of depends on you."

"What's that supposed to mean?"

"My stepping down comes with a cost, and you're the one who will have to pay."

"I'm listening."

"Good," Stone said. "Because I'm about to tell you some things that will give you a better understanding of why I am the way that I am. I'm hoping that understanding will make it easier for you to do what I'm going to ask you to do."

Valentine nodded. "Like I said, I'm listening."

For the next thirty minutes, Stone told him the bare-bones version of his warrior past. He avoided revealing any national security secrets, but supplied enough classified information to give Valentine a feel for things. He delved into his own psyche, explaining his belief that justice sometimes needed to be raw and primal, outside the constrictions of the law, which far too often failed.

When he was finished, he leaned back in his chair and waited for Valentine to say something.

The deputy took his time, seeming to take it all in, pondering, mulling things over. Finally, he broke his silence. "So, what you're telling me is that you're a vigilante."

"To put a name on it, yeah."

Valentine shook his head. "I can't believe there's an actual black ops trigger-puller living in my town, let alone wearing a badge and carrying a Bible."

"The badge wasn't planned. Things just worked out that way."

Valentine's eyes suddenly widened. "Wait a minute... did you have anything to do with Sheriff Camden's death?"

Stone fixed him with a frank, level gaze. "Camden died in a blizzard, eaten by coy-wolves. I think you can chalk that one up to God's justice, not mine."

"Not sure I believe you."

Stone shrugged. "Believe what you want. Whether I did it or God did it, the sick bastard had it coming."

"No argument from me," Valentine replied. "So, what is it you want from me in exchange for handing over the sheriff badge?"

"Cooperation."

"As far as what?"

"I may put down the badge," Stone said, "but I'm not putting down my guns."

Valentine quickly gleaned what he meant. "You're going to keep on killing."

"I'm going to keep on delivering justice when I think it's merited."

"You're playing semantics."

"And you've got a choice to make. Agree to work with me, and you can have this badge you want so badly. Or tell me you can't do that and I'll just hang onto the badge and go about business as usual."

Valentine said, "Or I could just have you arrested for all the murders you just confessed to."

"Did you forget that my black ops wet work was sanctioned by the government?"

"I'm not talking about those killings," Valentine replied cooly, an edge in his voice.

"Not sure what you think you heard, Cade, but I didn't confess to anything other than doing my job as a lawman."

"Right. By shooting, or stabbing, or burning, anyone you felt deserved it." Valentine shook his head. "A lawman is supposed to follow the *law,* Stone. It's right there in the title. You going all rogue whenever you feel like it is what makes me want to take that badge from you."

"So, take it," Stone said. He unpinned the badge and skidded it across the desk so that it stopped in front of the young deputy. "You worry about the law in this town and let me worry about justice."

"Not sure I can do that."

"Then elections are in November and may the best man win."

"I can't beat you and you know it."

"Then you have a hard decision to make."

"So, in order to become the sheriff, I have to agree to let a vigilante operate in my town with impunity."

"I'm not a psychopath, Cade," Stone said. "I'm not going to leave a trail of bodies like some kind of cowboy version of Jack the Ripper. Whether you admit it or not, you know that sometimes there are dirtbags out there who deserve greater punishment than the law allows. That's where I come in. Those are my targets."

Valentine shook his head again. "You're a preacher, for god's sake."

"I'm a lot of things," Stone replied. "But what I'm hoping to not be any longer is the Garrison County Sheriff." He reached over and tapped the badge lying between them. "What's it gonna be, Cade? You gonna pick this up, or do I need to put it back on?"

"Feels like I'm making a deal with the devil," the deputy muttered.

"I'm not the devil, and you know it."

"Yeah, well, you're no angel, either. Unless it's the angel of death."

"You've got a knack for hyperbole."

"And you've got a knack for stacking bodies."

"Guess you have to decide if you can live with it," Stone said.

"Even if I say yes, how do you know I'll honor the agreement?"

"Because I know that once you give your word on something, you keep it," Stone replied.

"I appreciate that."

"It's the truth."

Valentine stared at the badge for a long time. Stone waited, silent, letting the man think it through. He knew it was not a decision to be rushed.

Finally, the deputy nodded. "We have a deal."

"Mind me asking what made you decide to take it?"

"Drummond."

Stone arched his eyebrows, surprised to hear the name. Deputy Drummond had been assassinated by neo-Nazi terrorists a year and a half ago, on the orders of their leader, a man named Blake. Stone had ended up burying a knife in the guy's belly.

"We both know you could have just arrested Blake," Valentine said. "But you spilled his guts all over the snow instead."

Stone didn't say anything. No confirmation, no denial.

"Thing is," Valentine continued, "when I heard what you did, I was glad. Blake had his goon-squad beat me, then he murdered Drummond, and when you stabbed him, all I could think was, the son of a bitch got what he deserved. I was happy he died face down in his own stinking guts instead of rotting in a prison cell, wasting the taxpayers' money." The deputy sighed. "I don't want to be a hypocrite. I can't be happy you killed Blake but protest when you kill other pieces of garbage who deserve it just as much, if not more. But I do have one thing to ask before we shake hands on this."

"Go for it."

"If I have qualms about who you target, I want you to promise to hear me out and seriously consider my objections."

Stone didn't hesitate. "I'll hear you out, but the final decision is mine. I'm giving you the badge, but I'm not letting you put a leash on me. But you have my word that I'll always listen to what you have to say."

Valentine nodded and stuck out his hand. "Then we have a deal. I'll handle the law and order in this town, you'll do…whatever it is you do."

Stone shook his hand. "Whatever is necessary," he said. "That's what I do."

That evening, Stone sat on his back deck and watched the sun sink behind the jagged mountain peaks, dying rays burrowing into the bottom of the clouds and causing the sky to glow a brilliant burnt orange, as if the heavens were on fire. Sights like this were one of the many reasons he never doubted the presence of a Creator, a divine architect of the universe. He simply could not bring himself to believe that such spectacular displays of nature happened by chance, emerging by luck out of some primordial chaos, absent a guiding hand.

He picked up the glass of Jack and Coke, lots of ice,

easy on the Jack, sitting on the patio table next to him. He took a sip, smacked his lips appreciatively, and then set the drink back down before leaning over and rubbing Max's big, scarred-up head, making sure to get a good scratch behind the ears. The dog's back leg thumped against the deck in an involuntary display of satisfaction and affection.

"Gonna have to get used to having me around, boy," he said to the Shottie. "Not wearing that badge means I'll be home more."

Max chuffed at him as if to say, *Sounds good, but only if I get more biscuits.*

"Time to focus more on being a preacher," Stone said, talking to himself as much as the dog.

Of course, he knew that just because his priorities shifted to his spiritual duties, his code of primal justice wouldn't let him rest. He had tried to walk away from the killing to become a man of God, but really, all he had become was a man of God who killed. In medieval times, he would have been a warrior-priest, his lethal dispensations upon the wicked sanctioned by the church. And though civilized times had separated killers from clergymen, Stone could not deny the fact that he was a man of both faith and fury, and he was starting to come to terms with his dualistic—and arguably oxymoronic—nature.

His thoughts turned to Carson and Jenny. They were both orphans now, but in the midst of their loss, they seemed to have found each other. Obviously, it was far too soon to call it love. Emotions that flared up in the crucible often flamed out fast once things settled down. But Stone had a good feeling about the two teenagers and something in his gut told him their relationship would deepen and flourish.

If only he could say the same for him and Holly.

Just knowing they had hit a stumbling block hurt like

hell, but he vowed to do whatever it took to make things work. Love often came with a cost, and God knew a woman like Holly was worth fighting for.

As if sensing his thoughts, Max looked up and gave him a little bark that seemed to say, *Don't mess it up, buddy.*

Stone smiled and rubbed the dog's head. "Don't worry, pal, I'm not gonna lose her. We'll figure it out, I promise." He stood up and tossed the rest of his drink over the patio railing. "But first, I need to take a little road trip."

EPILOGUE

GADSBY LAKE, ALBERTA, CANADA

WHEN BILLIONAIRE HAROLD VACHEREAU had purchased the sprawling, three-hundred-acre lakeside estate for just shy of $20 million, the realtor had half-jokingly told him that the mansion was haunted. But so far, Vachereau had not seen any ghosts, no matter how many dead people he brought into the place.

The pitch-black night pushed against the rain-spattered windows, the moon hidden behind thick, swollen storm clouds that dumped a deluge on the ground below. The wind howled, turning the rain into liquid needles that lashed anything foolish enough to be caught outside.

Inside the opulent kitchen, Vachereau prepared a midnight feast, a dinner for one. He rarely indulged in this particular vice more than once or twice a month, and he never let his private chef prepare the food. No, the preparation was half the enjoyment, and he always undertook the task himself, and always late at night, while the house staff slept. Save for the security detail, of course, and they were under explicit instructions to never enter the kitchen at this hour.

He kept the lighting low to enhance the mood, and his frame cast a long, thin shadow across the mahogany floor of the dining room as he placed the meal on the table. Like everything else in the manor, the room reeked of decadence, from the crimson drapes to the rare paintings on the wall—he had a fondness for the work of Jean Paul Riopell—to the heavy chandelier that looked like it dripped with crystal tears. Harold Vachereau was not a man of subtle tastes.

He sat at the head of a table so large it could have handled Christ and all the apostles at the Last Supper and still had room left over. Any prick of conscience he had once felt at the taboo act in which he was about to indulge had long ago vanished. Somewhere along the way, he had convinced himself that, because of his vast wealth, the rules of normal society did not apply to him. Let the peasants scavenge for crumbs. The elite, such as himself, had more extravagant tastes that should not be denied.

His silk robe shimmered in the dim light as he uncorked a bottle of red wine, the scarlet liquid looking blood-hued as it poured into the glass. Before him, silver platters steamed with grotesque opulence: slabs of human flesh prepared in a variety of ways. Some roasted in a rosemary marinade, others pounded thin and lightly sauteed in garlic and butter, and yet another plate piled with raw, bite-sized chunks, perfect for dipping in the homemade ranch sauce he had whipped up earlier. He inhaled deeply. It all smelled so magnificently delicious.

Vachereau raised his glass to whatever ghosts might be lurking. "To indulgence," he murmured, his baritone voice thick with self-satisfaction. "To feasting on the forbidden and not giving a damn." He bitterly reflected that this might be his last meal of this nature for quite some time, since the pipeline he used to acquire his meat had been destroyed. It would take time to find another, but for people like him, money made everything possible. The demise of Rick and his cohorts was merely an unfortunate setback, nothing more.

A soft creak gave him pause.

He set down the glass and cocked his silver-haired head, listening intently. It didn't sound like the creak had come from the wind or the settling of old wood. No, it sounded like it came from much closer, inside the house.

Maybe the ghosts had come to pay him a visit after all.

"Someone there?" he called out, his voice brittle.

More silence. It lingered, ominous and pressing.

Then, from the far end of the dining room, a figure stepped into the light. Tall, rugged, eyes cold, wearing a flat-crowned Stetson with a rattlesnake band, rainwater dripping from the brim. "Yeah, I guess you could say someone's here," the intruder said.

Vachereau stayed seated, his obsidian eyes narrowing. "I know who you are." He made it sound like an accusation.

"Good," Stone said. "Saves me the bother of an introduction."

"How did you find me?"

"I have my ways."

"They must be very good. I take great steps and spend a lot of money to maintain my privacy."

"Not enough steps and not enough money, apparently."

"If you try to harm me, I will shout, and my guards will come running."

"Your guards are down for the count."

"Dead?"

Stone shook his head. "As far as I know, they were just doing their jobs. They'll wake up with headaches, but they'll wake up. I don't kill the innocent." He thrust his chin at the platters of human flesh. "Unlike you."

Vachereau made a scoffing sound deep in his throat. "The poor have always existed for the rich to feast upon. Besides, I may have blood on my lips, but none on my hands, as I have never killed anyone." He smiled, thin and cruel and utterly remorseless. "I pay others to do that."

Stone moved along the length of the table with the slow grace of a stalking wolf, his rubber-soled boots all but silent on the wooden floor. "Paying others doesn't cut you slack for your sins. You may not have held the knife, but you sure as hell have blood on your hands, Mr. Vachereau. Your wealth has shielded you until now, but it won't shield you from me."

The billionaire's face hardened. "I don't think you truly know who I am."

"I know *what* you are, and I know the world is better off without sick bastards like you in it."

As if to prove his point, Stone lifted the silver lid off a platter, exposing a row of human ribs, meat still clinging to the bone, lacquered in a dark glaze of barbecue sauce. With a look of disgust, he let the lid fall back into place, covering the ghastly cuisine.

Vachereau's eyes remained hard and unrepentant. "You call *sick* what you do not understand. Humans have devoured each other's flesh throughout history, and there is suppressed evidence that it not only bears significant health benefits, but life-expanding properties as well. Bottom line, Sheriff, or preacher, or whatever the hell you are, while it may be rare—no pun intended—it is hardly unprecedented."

"I'm not here for excuses," Stone said. "I'm here for justice."

"Justice for who?" Vachereau asked. "Certainly not for yourself. I've done nothing to you."

"For the dead," Stone replied.

"The dead don't care about justice."

"You're about to find out."

Vachereau abruptly stood up, knocking over his wine in the process. "You think you can skulk into my home and threaten me? I have half of Canada's politicians in my pocket and more Mounties at my beck and call than I know what to do with. Hell, I have the Prime Minister on speed dial."

"None of that is going to save you from me."

Outside, the wind howled like the voices of the damned.

Vachereau reached for the steak knife beside his plate. "You don't scare me."

Stone moved closer, his voice low and steady. "I'm not here to scare you. I'm here to end you."

Vachereau lunged, blade flashing. But Stone moved much faster. His hand came up holding a pistol equipped with a suppressor. He fired two bullets into the billionaire's guts. The knife clattered to the floor as Vachereau staggered back, clutching the oozing holes in his stomach. He could feel the much larger exit wounds in his back.

"Looks like you got a bellyache," Stone rasped. "Guess eating lead disagrees with you."

Vachereau slumped down in his chair. He knew that without medical attention, he would suffer a slow, agonizing death. "Please," he said. "For the love of God, call a doctor. I can pay you. Anything."

Stone stepped forward. "Oh, you're gonna pay all right."

He picked up the fork next to the dinner plate.

"No..." Vachereau begged.

His last words.

Stone rammed the fork into the hollow of the man's throat. A hot blast of air erupted from the torn trachea, causing blood to jet across the table. Stone watched as the cannibalistic billionaire thrashed and gurgled his way into oblivion.

Then he walked away and vanished back into the storm.

A LOOK AT: THE ASSASSIN'S PRAYER

THE ASSASSINS BOOK ONE

HARD-HITTING ACTION WITH A WHOLE LOT OF HEART.

Burned by the betrayal of his best friend and embittered by the tragic death of his wife, former government assassin Gabriel Asher becomes a freelance gun-for-hire, trying hard to bury the past beneath a violent sea of bullets, blood, and booze.

But some sins refuse to stay buried…

Asher soon finds himself targeted by Black Talon, a brutal kill-team from his past led by the ruthless and legendary Colonel Macklin. Asher just wants to be left alone but when fate thrusts an ex-lover back into his life and she is caught up in the crossfire, Asher unleashes a take-no-prisoners war against his enemies. As the guns thunder and the bodies bite the dust, he finds the scars on his soul being ripped wide open.

With its full-throttle pace, hard-hitting action, and heart-wrenching emotion, The Assassin's Prayer is a relentless tale of redemption for those who know that sometimes bullets speak louder than words.

Publisher's Note: The Assassin's Prayer has been updated with new characters, major revisions, and an exhilarating new ending in this brand-new edition.

AVAILABLE NOW

THANK YOU

Thank you for taking the time to read *Hell's Harvest*. If you enjoyed it, please consider telling your friends or posting a short review. Word of mouth is an author's best friend and much appreciated.

Thank you.
Mark Allen

ABOUT THE AUTHOR

Mark Allen was raised by an ancient clan of ruthless ninjas—though breaking his oath of silence to say so might get him killed. When not practicing shuriken throws or hunting flea markets for a katana, Mark writes high-octane action fiction. He calls it "guns 'n' guts"—packed with twin Micro-Uzis, headshots galore, and punchy prose.

He wrote his first story at 16, won a regional contest soon after, and later published *The Assassin's Prayer,* which sold over 10,000 copies in its first year. Originally optioned by Showtime, the novel blends raw emotion with brutal action, earning Mark a loyal readership.

He lives in the Adirondacks with a skeptical wife, two martial arts–averse daughters, and enough firepower to keep door-to-door salesmen at bay.

www.ingramcontent.com/pod-product-compliance
Lightning Source LLC
LaVergne TN
LVHW030919080826
845145LV00013B/2967

9781685497552